Sunlight on a Broken Column

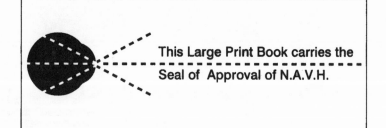

Sunlight on a Broken Column

Catherine M. Rae

Thorndike Press • Thorndike, Maine

Published in 1998 by arrangement with St. Martin's Press, Inc.

Thorndike Large Print ® Basic Series.

The tree indicium is a trademark of Thorndike Press.

The text of this Large Print edition is unabridged.
Other aspects of the book may vary from the original edition.

Set in 16 pt. Plantin.

Printed in the United States on permanent paper.

Library of Congress Cataloging in Publication Data

Rae, Catherine M., 1914–
    Sunlight on a broken column / Catherine M. Rae.
      p. cm.
    ISBN 0-7862-1316-7 (lg. print : hc : alk. paper)
    1. Large type books.   I. Title.
  [PS3568.A355S86   1998]
  813'.54—dc21   97-43484

for Cathy

Part I

Caroline

Chapter 1

The day we moved out of the old house on Harrison Street in downtown New York I tripped over the loose board in the front hall and cut my forehead on the edge of the small marble shelf meant for letters and calling cards. I had run back in from the waiting cab to coax Caesar, our large black-and-white cat of indeterminate age, from behind the kitchen stove, where he had taken refuge from the confusion caused by our departure. Like most cats, he disliked any interruption to his daily schedule, and besides, the noise made by the men who came for our trunks and cases as they tramped through the house probably hurt his ears.

That is why I fell: The rug in the hall had been taken up, the one Mamma bought to cover the place where my brother Jeremy had pried up a piece of parquet when he was little. He said he needed it for a boat he was making, but I know that he did it because he was in a temper at not being allowed to go over to the docks on the Hudson River with his friends.

"I've wanted a rug there for years, anyway," Mamma said airily when Papa asked her why she hadn't called the carpenter to repair the damage, "and it covers it so nicely."

Papa sighed, but after warning Jeremy against any further desecration of the house, let the matter rest. He never could say no to Mamma. He wasn't quite so amicable, though, when he saw me climb into the cab with blood dripping down over my cheek and Caesar clutched in my arms.

"Damn that cat!" he exploded. "He's nothing but one hell of a nuisance! Couldn't you have left him for the Conklins? They'll be moving in tomorrow. And what will you do with him in the new house?"

"Now, Samuel," Mamma said placatingly, "you know we'll need a cat wherever we live. There isn't a house in New York that doesn't have mice, and I'm simply terrified of the filthy things."

"Oh, very well," Papa said resignedly as he turned to me. "Caroline, stop that sniveling. You're upsetting your mother. That little cut can't be so painful. Here, take my handkerchief and mop up your face. Go on, driver."

He was wrong on two counts: First, he was the one who was upset, and second, I wasn't crying on account of the cut, but because we were leaving 314 Harrison Street, the only home I had ever known, and I dreaded living in the great, cold, stone mansion on Sixty-eighth Street.

My siblings took a more cheerful view of the move. Of course, they were older than I was. At that time, the fall of 1892, Brad, at twenty-two, was reading law at the firm of Lewis, Crouch, and Fisk (Mr. Fisk was an old friend of Papa's) and hoping to marry Elspeth Dowd in the near future. Jeremy, two years younger, was limping through Columbia College, undecided on a career.

Laurel, the beauty of the family, was eighteen, and had already had two proposals of marriage, both of which Papa had rejected. Everyone adored Laurel; even I, jealous little beast that I was, had to admire her. She seemed to have everything. As Mamma was fond of saying, the gods must have been smiling when she was born. Her long blond hair curled just enough to make it manageable, her brown eyes were flecked with gold (gold dust, to quote Mamma again), and her complexion had all the freshness and delicacy of the camellias I saw in the florist's window on Chambers Street. Next to Laurel

11

I felt that I looked like one of the homemade rag dolls that old Miss Cooker in Number 212 used to make for the Christmas bazaar at the church.

I never understood how Laurel invariably managed to appear looking so lovely; she didn't spend hours at our small dressing table, but I noticed that she was careful never to leave our room without a glance in the long mirror that hung on the back of our closet door. She told me she had to make sure her skirt was hanging properly, and that all her buttons and snappers were fastened.

She was not only neat about her appearance, but also about her possessions: Her collection of small objects, a silver thimble (although to my knowledge she never sewed a stitch), a lovely, smooth marble egg, a miniature Limoges tea set, and a tiny wooden model of a sailing ship, were all carefully wrapped in tissue paper and stored in a Christmas box that had come from A. T. Stewart's Emporium. There were undoubtedly other things that I've forgotten, but I do remember Mamma saying Laurel was never a problem when it came to birthday presents. "Just give her a silver cat or a golden mouse for her treasure chest," she'd say, "and Laurel will love you."

I've often wondered what became of all

those little objects — I haven't seen them in years.

At the time of our move uptown (everyone who was anyone in New York in 1892 was moving north, according to Papa) I was an awkward, skinny seventeen-year-old with straight brown hair, uninteresting greenish brown eyes, and a tendency to blush painfully. Mamma and Laurel did the best they could with me, but dresses never seemed to hang properly on my bony body, and even if I slept (or tried to sleep) all night with my head in rag curlers, my hair would be hanging down limply by the time breakfast was over. I finally took to wearing it parted in the middle and pulled back into an untidy bun. In a daguerreotype taken about that time I resembled a young girl in an early American painting I'd seen in one of Papa's books. She is by no means a beauty, but she has a look, an expression in her eyes that seems to be asking questions, the kind of look that is apt to irritate grown-ups.

I had seen our new home once before, but

only from the outside. Mamma had taken Laurel and me up to Sixty-eighth Street in a cab one afternoon and had us driven slowly past it. She pointed with pride to the impressive entrance (seven wide stone steps leading up to a massive front door instead of the three narrow ones we had in Harrison Street), counted the windows (nineteen in all instead of eight), and exclaimed over the solid stone railing that surrounded the areaway on either side of the stoop, almost hiding four additional windows in the basement.

"Think of it, girls," she said, clasping and unclasping her hands in her excitement, "a drawing room, reception room, formal dining room, library, morning room — oh, I forget what else!"

"And separate bedrooms for Caroline and me?" Laurel asked.

"Bedrooms galore," Mamma replied. "And even dressing rooms as well as two upstairs sitting rooms. Oh, I can't wait until we're settled there!"

She had never complained about the lack of luxury during our years in Harrison Street, but it was obvious that she was looking forward to a life that Papa's newly acquired wealth would provide. He'd recently been made an officer (executive vice president, I think) of the bank in which he'd worked ever since he was a boy, starting as a messenger and moving up steadily. His father had been president of that bank years ago, and that may have had something to do with his unusually rapid rise.

As I remember, it was in 1890 that money began to be more plentiful than it had been earlier. We had more new dresses for one thing, and Mamma began to wear jewelry, but it was not until '92 that Papa declared himself "a rich man." At the time I had no idea where the money came from, and it was not until years later that I learned about the enormous financial risks he took. He couldn't have looked upon them as risks, though, because instead of worrying about his investments he boasted happily about the "killings" he made in the stock market. More than once I heard him urge Mamma to buy anything she wanted for the house: "Don't even think of economizing, my dear," he'd say. "I have enough money to buy a dozen houses now. Get whatever your heart desires." She did, too.

In the days that followed our trip uptown I brooded unhappily over the move, but I knew better than to tell Mamma, or anyone else in the family, that I had disliked the mansion on sight, that something about it frightened me, and that I would much rather stay in our neat little two-and-a-half-story brick house.

The nine houses that made up the L-shaped enclave encompassing Washington and Harrison Streets were almost identical, each with its modest front door and the aforementioned eight windows, two of which were dormers. They were simple houses, the kind a child in kindergarten would draw on a slate. There were no bay windows, and except for the fanlights over the front doors, no ornamentation of any kind. I loved them. Ours, known as the Jonas Wood house, had been built in 1804, and with the exception of the addition of a bathroom and new appointments in the kitchen, very few changes had been made over the years.

There are those who hold that large rooms are easier to maintain than small ones, but I do not agree with that. The somewhat cluttered parlor we had struck me as being the perfect size, at least for our family. It held the six of us comfortably, and if Mamma entertained, the sliding doors between it and the dining room could be thrown open. She didn't entertain frequently in those days, though; she was too busy raising us, she said.

We didn't have much household help at that time, just Molly, a sort of maid of all work, who cooked (unless Mamma decided to produce something special for dinner) and cleaned, and a laundress who came in one day a week. Ordinarily, our dinners were not fancy, consisting as they did of meat, potatoes, and whatever vegetable was available. How I loathed the turnips that showed up on the table so often during the winter months! I also became tired of apple pie, which the boys clamored for, and which we had for dessert three or four times a week. We certainly were not living in the lap of luxury, but it was the only life I had ever known, and I resented having to leave it.

To make matters worse, none of the old familiar furnishings were to go to our new home. They would not be suitable, according to Mr. Colby of W. and J. Sloane. He was undoubtedly right; the chairs and sofa, while comfortable, were worn, and I had to agree that the lamp tables looked ready for a secondhand furniture store once the covers we kept on them had been removed. All the same, I objected to Mr. Colby's casual dismissal of articles I'd lived with for so long. It was like abandoning old friends.

Friends! That was another thing: The only

real friends I had lived in our enclave, and while Mamma promised that I'd be able to keep in touch with them, I knew that once we were in Sixty-eighth Street the old intimacy would be lost. There'd be no more knocking on Sarah Makin's door to find out if she'd walk down to the milliner's with me, no more impromptu tea parties with the Ambrose girls, and worst of all, no more late afternoon walks with Peter Aspinwall after his classes at Columbia were over for the day. Sixty-eighth Street did not look like the kind of street where neighbors knew each other, much less fraternized.

"You're making yourself miserable over nothing, Caroline," Mamma said when I complained about being cut off from people I'd known for years. "You would do well to follow Laurel's example; she's looking forward to new experiences, to meeting new people, to a whole new way of life. Why can't you adopt that attitude?"

I'm not Laurel, I thought. I'm not like her in any way. She's pretty and I'm plain; she'll go to parties and dances and I'll stay home with a book, and she'll make a brilliant marriage while I'll be a spinster forever. Even Peter Aspinwall wouldn't marry me, and he's no great catch.

When the cab drew up in front of 7 East Sixty-eighth Street on the day of the move, I had to admit that it looked more welcoming than it had when Mamma first showed it to us. Of course, it had been empty then, with the bleak look that hovers over unoccupied houses, and now heavy lace curtains hung at the nineteen windows and some sort of greenery had been planted in the large stone box in the enclosure over the front door, while clumps of late fall flowers bloomed in the window box to the left of the stoop.

My entrance to our new home was no more graceful than my exit from the old one had been: Caesar, no doubt as unhappy as I was, squirmed out of my arms as I crossed the threshold, causing me to stumble over him as I leaned down to catch him. In trying to save myself from falling, I caught hold of the nearest object to me, a huge Chinese jardiniere. I don't know which noise was the louder, the crash of the china or Papa's voice when he shouted:

"For God's sake, Caroline! What has come over you today?"

Chapter 2

Not surprisingly, I was the only member of the family who did not adjust well to our new surroundings. Laurel, Brad, and Jeremy might have been born to the luxury with which we were suddenly surrounded — the maids, the butler, the cook, and all the accoutrements of wealth. The silks and velvets, the tapestries and embroideries, to say nothing of the massive pieces of furniture Sloane's and Mr. Colby had chosen, may have been suitable for the mansion, but I found them overwhelming.

One by one I removed from my room as many of the little pillows and ornaments as I dared, secreting them in the back of the linen press at the end of the upstairs hall. I could do nothing about the large armoire or the oversized canopied bed, but after I took down the portrait of a simpering female that hung over my fireplace and snipped off the fringe at the edges of my draperies I felt that I could tolerate, if not like, the room. In fact, I came to enjoy spending an evening in front of the small fire in the grate with Caesar purring in his basket beside my chair. He spent most of his time in my room, going down to the kitchen for food only at stated intervals. Then Mrs. Ellis, the cook, who fortunately liked cats, would let him out into the garden for what she called his "airing."

Since my room was in the rear of the building, overlooking the back garden, I could watch him as he prowled among the bushes and shrubs. If I tapped on the glass, his ears would perk up, and in a moment or two his yellow-green eyes would be staring at me. From that same window I could see the house directly behind us, the garden of which was separated from ours by a waist-high stone wall. I was interested in what I could see of that house because it looked so much like our own, at least from the rear. The similarity of the two structures was so striking that when I walked around the block to view the Sixty-ninth Street house from the front, I was not surprised to see that it was practically a duplicate of ours.

It is true that our neighbor's house was somewhat smaller, having only three floors above the basement instead of our four, but the entire design, the stoop, the entrance, the arrangement of the windows, and most of the architectural details were exact duplicates. Even the decorative stone railings that ran around the edges of the roofs were identical.

I was standing on the north side of Sixty-ninth Street staring at our near double when a face appeared in the bay window on the second floor in what would would be the equivalent of Mamma's sitting room. I turned and started to walk toward Fifth Avenue, thinking that whoever it was would motion to me to go away, the way old Mrs. Shelbourne used to do when we played some noisy game in front of her house on Harrison Street. I was wrong: When I looked up at the window again it had been thrown open, and an elderly woman with a lace cap on her head leaned out. I couldn't hear what she said, but from her gestures it was clear that she wanted me to cross the street and knock on her front door. When I nodded that I understood, she clapped her hands and closed the window quietly.

Why did I answer her summons so readily, without hesitating for a moment, or even wondering why she wanted to see me? I didn't stop to think that it might be unusual, even peculiar, for a complete stranger to be invited off the street into one of the city's grandest houses. Was it boredom with the dull life I was now leading, or merely curiosity? No, I think it was not either of those, but rather the authoritative way in which the old lady had commanded me to come to her.

A tall, rather muscular but neatly dressed manservant — he didn't look quite like a butler — answered my ring and led me up a flight of marble stairs, exactly like ours except for the color of the carpeting, to the second floor.

"Come in, come in," an impatient voice cried out even before the man had finished knocking. "Come over here, girl, where I can see you, and Gordon, go see about tea! Tea at once! And make sure there are madeleines today."

The man Gordon withdrew silently, closing the door carefully behind him. My hostess, who was sitting erect in a large, velvet-covered wing chair near the window, held out a small, soft hand for me to take. She wore no rings, and when I looked up I saw that her only jewelry was a diamond and amethyst pin at her throat.

"I know who you are," she said suddenly. "I have seen you in your garden. I do not, however, know your name."

"I am Caroline Slade," I said in response

to the implied question.

"And I am Henrietta Prentice," she said briskly. "Prentice is spelled i-c-e, not i-s-s; Miss Henrietta Prentice, of a long line of New York Prentices."

"How do you do, Miss Prentice," I said, feeling as if I ought to make a deep curtsey. "I am very happy to meet you. I have admired your beautiful garden."

"Oh, the garden," she said with a dismissive wave of her hand. "That's Leland's doing. He's my nephew; he lives here."

At that point there was a knock on the door and two maids wheeled in a table bearing an incredibly lovely silver tea service as well as plates of tiny sandwiches and little delicacies which I thought must be the requested madeleines. Years later, when I read Proust, I had to smile at the recollection of that extremely neat and proper old lady as she ignored the sandwiches and concentrated almost greedily on those delectable shell-shaped morsels.

"I suppose you are wondering why the two houses are so much alike, Miss Slade," Miss Prentice said after the tea had been poured and the maids were gone. "That's why you were standing out in the street, isn't it?"

"Yes, ma'am," I replied. "I could tell from the rear windows —"

"Of course you could," she interrupted impatiently. "Anyone could. And I suppose you want to know why, don't you? And who was responsible for two such extravaganzas in such poor taste?"

"I am interested —"

"Naturally you are, since you live in one of them. Well, there is a simple explanation: My father had them both built. He commissioned a Boston firm of architects, Brownlow and Hodge, to design them more than forty years ago. They were to be identical, but after the first one was finished — the one you are living in — something went wrong in the financial world, and because of the heavy expenses involved, this one had to be somewhat modified. Father was unhappy about that . . ."

Miss Prentice's voice trailed off at that point, and she seemed lost in thought for a minute before giving a little laugh and continuing:

"On the other hand, he was inordinately proud of his 'connection,' even though Mother teased him about it. I remember her saying, 'James, you're a hopeless romantic! You never should have read *The Mysteries of Udolpho* and those other Gothic novels with all their secret underground passages. What on earth will you think of next?'

"Oh, excuse me, my dear! I've been rambling. Where was I? Oh, yes, after a while Father made another fortune, but by that time it was too late; all the work had been completed. But this house was always a disappointment to him; you see, yours was for my sister, Lavinia, and this one for me, and he was worried that I would feel slighted. I must admit that I did, a bit, but in the end I fared better than poor Lavinia."

"What happened to her, Miss Prentice?" I asked when she paused.

"She married Bruce Kendrick — why, I cannot imagine — when she was only seventeen, and died a year later giving birth to a daughter. Puerperal fever, the doctor said. Her daughter, Sybil, grew up in that house with nurses and governesses hired by her father. Then Sybil married young, and like her mother, died in childbed, leaving the infant Leland. His father, Walter Bigelow, brought the baby over to me, and then took whatever money and valuables he could lay his hands on and went off. You see, Sybil's fortune was secured in a trust for Leland, and there was no way Walter Bigelow could get at it. I heard he died out west some years ago. Leland has been living with me ever since then, twenty-eight years now."

"What happened to his grandfather, Mr.

Kendrick?" I asked as she picked up her teacup and sat back in the huge chair.

"Oh, he stayed in the house, your house, until he drank himself to death. After that the building was sold. What would Leland and I want with two houses?"

"Then your nephew's name is Leland Bigelow?" I asked after a moment or two of silence.

"Oh, no, mercy no," she answered quickly. "As soon as I could I had it legally changed to Prentice; he has been Leland Prentice since he was less than a year old. Now, enough of my family, my dear. Tell me about yours."

I had meant to ask her to explain what her father's "connection" was, and later on I dearly wished I had, but she kept me talking about the Slades until it was time for me to leave.

"She seemed so anxious for company, Mamma," I said that evening when she and I were alone in the drawing room. Papa was out at some political dinner or other, Brad had gone to see Elspeth, Laurel had been invited to the opera, and Jeremy was upstairs studying, or pretending to study. I had been

27

surprised to see him carrying a copy of Mr. Stevenson's new book, *The Strange Case of Dr. Jekyll and Mr. Hyde*, up with him. He rarely read anything but biographies of famous men, and lately he'd been concentrating on Mr. Lincoln and the heroes of the Civil War.

"I'm sure Miss Prentice would welcome a visit from you, Mamma," I said when my mother remained silent.

"Well, perhaps I will call on her, dear," she said vaguely. "I'm so busy, though. So many calls to make, so many appointments, and then there's Laurel's new gown to see to — the one for the Assembly Ball next week. She is so looking forward to it. I do wish you'd come with us, Caroline. You'd meet some lovely young people, I'm sure."

"No, Mamma, I won't. I'd just be a wallflower, and bored to death," I said firmly.

"But Caroline," she pleaded, "you must do *something*. You simply cannot just mope around the house, lovely as it is, and do nothing. What am I to do with you?"

I had no answer for her; I had no idea what I was going to do with myself at that time, but a few days later when I was out for one of my solitary walks, I passed the huge, cathedral-like brick building on Park Avenue that housed the Normal College. When I paused for a moment to look up at it, the large doors at the top of the steps swung open and a stream of laughing, chattering young women poured out and down onto Park Avenue.

I thought at first they were all wearing some kind of uniform, but on taking a closer look I could see slight, very slight, variations in their dress. Their long dark skirts, some brown, some black, came down to their ankles, and short, fitted jackets were worn over what looked like starched white shirtwaists. Most of them seemed to be about my age, and when one, a very pretty girl, smiled at me, I was emboldened to ask her what the Normal College was like. She and her companion seemed somewhat startled by my question, but after some hesitation they both laughed and began to speak at once.

"It's like any other school, I guess," the pretty one said, "except that you're supposed to know how to teach children their lessons when you graduate."

"That's it," the second girl agreed. "They teach you how to teach, or you hope they do so that you'll get a position in a school. Look, if you want to know all about it, why don't you go in and see Miss Atkinson? She was still in her office when I went by. It's just to the right as you go in.

Come on, Polly, or we'll be late."

I thanked them and watched them hurry around the corner of Sixty-eighth Street toward Lexington Avenue. I was wondering what it was they might be late for as I turned and slowly mounted the stone steps of that somewhat forbidding building.

Chapter 3

"You've done what?" Mamma asked sharply, placing her knife and fork carefully on her dinner plate and fixing her eyes on me. "Did I hear you say you had enrolled in a school so that you can learn how to teach children their ABCs? I cannot countenance such a thing! Why on earth — Samuel, please be good enough to speak to her!"

Before Papa could say anything, Jeremy, who sat across the table from me, clapped his hands and smiled.

"Good for you, Caro," he said, nodding approval. "That's great! It's time one of us started on a career. I'm going to —"

"Never mind your future right now, Jeremy," Papa interrupted. "It's Caroline's that is under consideration."

He turned to look at me for a moment before he spoke, and when he did his voice was gentle. "Is this some whim, child, or have you given it serious thought?"

"You can't be serious, Caro," Laurel said in the indulgent tone one would use with a child. "You might as well study to become a maid, or a cook, and why on earth would you do that?"

"I am serious, Papa," I said. "I really want —"

"Of all the ridiculous —" Mamma stopped suddenly when Papa put up his hand for silence.

"Caroline," he said quietly, "I will see you in the library after dinner. Right now I would like to know what plans the rest of you have for the evening. Jeremy?"

In spite of Mamma's objections, my father consented to my attending the Normal College, but not until he had carefully read the brochure I handed him listing the course of studies for the first term.

"Well," he said, sitting back comfortably in his large leather armchair, "this can't do you any harm, Caroline, and it may very well do you some good. And it seems that it is entirely tuition free. Which language will you elect, French or German?"

"German, I think, Papa. I used to like the stories and legends Mrs. Hoffenberger told us when she came to do the dressmaking down in Harrison Street."

"Good," he said. "And what about Latin, ancient history, algebra, and plane geometry? Do you think you can handle all of them?"

"I don't see why not," I answered with more confidence than I felt. "If all those girls I saw can . . ." I let the rest of the sentence die out. "But of course I can't start until September, and it's only the middle of May now, so that gives me three and a half months to do some reading. I think Jeremy has a few ancient history books."

"Very well, then," he said, closing the little blue-covered manual I'd given him to look at and handing it back to me. "Go ahead with it, my dear, and let me see some of your work from time to time, at the end of each week, perhaps."

"Thank you, Papa. And you'll make it all right with Mamma, then?"

"Yes. Leave your mother to me, but, Caroline, do try to please her. Take an interest in clothes and things; you know the sorts of things she likes to talk about. Now, run along, my dear. I have some papers here that need my attention."

I wondered what he would say to placate my mother, and was rather surprised when

Jeremy knocked on my door the following evening to tell me that he'd overheard Papa say to her that he thought the Normal College would "bring me out of myself," whatever that might mean.

"Go to Papa when you want something," my brother continued, lingering in front of my bookcase and running his fingers across the titles. "He's more reasonable than Mamma. Oh, I don't mean that she's really *un*reasonable — it's just that she's not interested in anything that doesn't have to do with clothes and social events. Too boring. Papa's interested in everything. Just keep this cat out of his way, and you'll have him on your side." With that he rubbed Caesar's head, waved at me, and took his leave.

Jeremy was right: Later that week when I received a formal invitation to have tea with Miss Prentice, Papa was far more interested in what I had to say about her than Mamma had been (she'd never found the time to call on the old lady).

"So that's the story behind these houses!" he exclaimed. "Of course you must accept, Caroline. Maybe Miss Prentice will have more to tell you about their history. And I think you'll do her good. It sounds to me as if the poor woman is hungry for company. What about the nephew? Have you met him?"

"No," I replied, "but I've seen him occasionally from my window. He walks around the garden in the late afternoon, smoking a cigar. Miss Prentice said the garden was his doing, but actually they have a man, a gardener, I suppose, who does all the digging and planting."

"Well, of course," Mamma broke in. "That's what we do. I decide what flowers and shrubs I want and Murphy plants them."

"What does he look like, this nephew?" Laurel asked.

"I couldn't see his face too clearly," I replied, "but he's tall, about Brad's height, and he wears gray suits and one of those Panama hats, and Miss Prentice said he's twenty-eight years old."

"Maybe he'll be at the tea party tomorrow," she said with a smile. "Size him up for me, Caro."

"Laurel, Laurel," Papa said, shaking his head in mock exasperation. "Haven't you enough beaux without scouring the neighborhood for more?"

"I am happy to see that you are punctual, my dear," Miss Prentice greeted me when I was shown into her sitting room promptly at four o'clock the next day. "So many people nowadays think it is fashionable to be late! So rude of them to keep the hostess waiting!"

I was no sooner seated than tea was brought in, this time with an array of varicolored petits fours in addition to the paperthin sandwiches and madeleines, as well as a third cup and saucer. Apparently someone else was expected.

"Will you be going away for the summer?" I asked when the tea had been poured.

"Oh, mercy, yes!" she exclaimed. "In fact, I'll be leaving for Newport shortly. We never spent the hot weather in the city when I was growing up. My mother simply wilted in the heat, so Father built a cottage on the waterfront for her. Corinth, he called it; he loved Greece. It's nothing pretentious, mind you, just a summer place, but with all the conveniences. You must come and visit me if you can."

"I'd love to, Miss Prentice, but we generally go to Shelter Island."

"Oh, well, in that case . . . I suppose you'll close up the city house? I am fortunate enough not to have to bother with that. Leland stays in town — I cannot understand why. He loves the garden here, but he has no use for country places! What do you make of that?"

"What should she make of it, Aunt?" asked a voice from the doorway. "She neither knows me —"

"Oh, Leland dear, come in. This is Miss Caroline Slade. My nephew, Leland Prentice, Miss Slade."

We nodded to each other, and as he approached the tea table I noticed that he walked with a slight, very slight, limp, which had not been apparent the few times I'd seen him in the garden.

"I've been admiring that handsome cat of yours, Miss Slade," he said with a smile when he was settled in the the petit point chair positioned between myself and Miss Prentice. "He sits on the top of the wall and keeps an eye on me when I'm out in the garden. What is his name?"

"Caesar, Mr. Prentice, because of the way he walks around as if he owned an empire. But he's really quite a gentle cat. I hope he doesn't bother you."

"No, no, of course he doesn't. He amuses

me. He seems to be listening carefully when I say hello and ask him how the world is treating him. Aunt, you should get a cat. They're fascinating to watch, and good company, too."

"I know, Leland, I know," Miss Prentice said with a sigh. "We always had cats when your grandmother and I were growing up, but now — I don't know. I am afraid I might trip over one; you know how they appear out of nowhere when you least expect them."

She went on to tell a story about a cat who had caused one of the maids to stumble and drop a tray set with her mother's best china, how the cat yowled and the maid had hysterics, and how her mother cried. While she was talking I glanced at her nephew. The expression on his face was one of affectionate, amused interest, although I had the feeling that this was not the first time he'd heard the story. I liked his manner, and I liked his appearance, the kind gray eyes, the wide mouth that seemed to turn up ever so slightly at the corners as if ready to smile, the light brown hair, and ears that clung close to his head. He's almost handsome, I thought, almost . . .

When it came time for me to leave, instead of ringing for the butler as Miss Prentice requested, Leland stood up and asked permission to see me home himself. Miss Prentice looked surprised, but she merely nodded graciously and wished me a pleasant summer. When I turned to wave to her from the doorway, she looked so frail and wistful behind the tea table that I wondered if she hadn't been counting on a longer visit from her nephew.

"It's kind of you to visit my aunt, Miss Slade," he said when we were out on Sixty-ninth Street. "Few people do, and she doesn't go out at all these days."

"Is she ill, Mr. Prentice?" I asked.

"It's more a matter of vanity than of illness," he said with a smile. "Because of the rheumatism in her legs, the doctor forbade her to go out without either a companion or a walking stick to aid her. She flatly refused to consider either one, saying that she could never tolerate the pitying glances that were sure to be cast her way. I rather admire her spirit, even though her stubbornness has severely limited her activities."

I rather admire her, too, I thought, but I couldn't help wondering if during her stay in Newport, far away from her doctor and the city streets, the strong-minded old lady didn't do exactly as she pleased.

"I'll certainly call on her when summer is

over and we're all back in the city," I said as we paused in front of our stoop. "Thank you for seeing me home, Mr. Prentice," I added as he stood looking down at me. "It was most kind of you."

"A pleasure, Miss Slade," he said, bowing slightly before turning away.

Wait until he sees Laurel, I thought as I mounted the steps. He'll never look at me again.

Although an entire winter and spring had elapsed since our move from Harrison Street, it seemed to me that we had barely settled into the new house when we were packing up again to go away for the summer. Ordinarily, as I had told Miss Prentice, we spent the hot weather on Shelter Island in a modest shingled house my father rented for the season. Other than walks through the wooded areas, berry picking expeditions, and the daily swim in the bay, there was little to do in that quiet retreat. Papa would come down from the city for weekends and organize outings to the mainland, but during the rest of the time we would all, as Mamma liked to say, vegetate in the sun.

Since Papa had become so wealthy, however, Shelter Island would no longer suffice. Laurel suggested that we go to Bar Harbor; Brad voted for Southampton, where Elspeth Dowd's family had a summer home; Jeremy suggested an extended trip through the South, during which we would visit Gettysburg, Appomattox, and various other Civil War battlegrounds. I said I'd like to go to London to see the famous tower in which Sir Walter Raleigh had been imprisoned, although I knew full well we'd never get Papa that far away from his office.

In the end, as we all expected, Mamma made the decision. At her instigation, a "cottage" was rented in the Berkshires, not far from the famous Shadowbrook, the one-hundred-room castle built by Anson Phelps Stokes.

"Our cottage," Mamma said happily, "has enough rooms to accommodate any number of your friends, and not only that, but a stable of horses for riding! Plus carriages, tennis and croquet courts, and ever so many extras! It will be a summer to remember!"

And so it was, but not in the way she visualized.

"Don't look so down in the mouth, Jeremy," Papa said when Mamma stopped listing the advantages of a season in the Berkshires. "You, at least, will get part of your

41

heart's desire. Before we go to the Berkshires I must make a trip to Washington on some business for the bank involving government pensions. Your mother will accompany me since there will be several social functions I must attend, and I thought that you and Caroline might come along. It would be educational for both of you. You'll be able to see several historic points of interest, Lee's house in Arlington, Mount Vernon, and so on."

Jeremy, of course, was delighted at the prospect, but while I was pleased at being included, I was not wildly excited at first. When Papa said that some of his business would entail a visit to Ford's Theater, where Lincoln was shot by John Wilkes Booth, and which now housed the offices of the Bureau of Records and Pensions, my brother began preparing himself to give us a guided tour through what was left of the theater. Mamma smiled at Jeremy indulgently, but I could only picture myself tagging along after him like a well-trained puppy. Papa knew better than to suggest that Laurel accompany us.

My father's enthusiasm, however, was contagious, and before the week was out I found myself looking forward to the long train trip, eating lunch in the luxurious dining car while watching the countryside slide past, and then curling up with a book in the large parlor car "chair" afterward. Everyone in the family seemed happy just then, and I remember experiencing a feeling of warmth and appreciation for my parents when I saw Papa nod approvingly as Mamma described the effect the news of Lincoln's death had had not only on her family but also on all New York.

"The entire city went into mourning," she said with a slight quaver in her voice. "Of course I was young at the time, but even so I felt crushed, devastated. What would we do without him, we wondered — oh, it was a terrible time!"

She sighed, but a moment or two later she brightened up and, looking around the table at us, began to talk about how we'd see lots of beautiful sights and splendid homes.

"Yes, indeed, my dear," Papa said when she paused. "And I've already made arrangements for a trip out to Mount Vernon, so you will be able to see the mansion of our first president."

"I'm beginning to wish I were going with you," Brad said shaking his head. "I don't dare take the time off now, though."

"Never mind, Brad dear," Mamma said, leaning over to pat his hand. "We'll bring you a present, something special. And one for you, too, Laurel."

Laurel, who had been quiet throughout the meal, smiled happily now. She knew how generous, even extravagant, Mamma could be, and was probably looking forward to a gold bracelet or necklace. Brad, on the other hand, would be content with a book or even a small souvenir.

I didn't realize it then, when we were gathered around the dinner table, but I now know both our parents were doing their best to prepare the four of us for our adult lives, and I am grateful to them, if only in retrospect. I am glad, though, that they never knew what was in store for us.

Unfortunately the high spirits with which we started out on the morning of June 8, 1893, did not last. The train to Washington was several hours late arriving at the Union Station, the accommodations at the hotel (I've forgotten the name of it) were not at all comfortable, and the heat of the city was more oppressive than anything I had ever felt.

"Cheer up," Papa said as we waited for a cab to take us to Ford's Theater the morning after our arrival. "I've made arrangements to move over to the Willard Hotel later today. We'll be much better off there."

"I certainly hope so, Samuel," Mamma said crossly. "I had hardly a wink of sleep last night. That bed was impossible. I hope the Willard has better mattresses. And this heat! Why, it's only the ninth of June! Not even summer yet. How do the people who live here stand it?"

We never saw the Willard Hotel, nor did I ever see my parents alive again after they were escorted into the pension offices, leaving Jeremy and me to wander around the parts of the building that were open to the public. I trailed after my brother for a while, looking at bits of Lincoln memorabilia, but the air in the building was so heavy that after a while I left him, saying I would go across the street to look at the Peterson house, where the president had actually died.

I remember that I was studying the marble plaque in memory of Lincoln's death, the one that Congress had affixed to the outside of the house, when I heard a strange rumbling sound, and then suddenly a tremendous blast that caused me to grasp the railing on the side of the steps for support. Three stories of Ford's Theater had collapsed, killing twenty-three people, my parents among them, and seriously injuring my brother. He died that night in Columbia Hospital.

I felt as though I were only half alive after my return to New York with Brad and Laurel. Full realization of the extent of the tragedy did not come immediately; I think I was in some sort of state of despair or shock, unable to accept what had happened, unable to mourn for my parents and brother, unable to cry.

Later, though, when the tears did come, they were almost uncontrollable. Brad said I cried for three weeks at least, and that may be true because I remember vowing that I would be serene, calm, and reasonable and then bursting into tears at the sight of one of Mamma's potpourris or Papa's silver-banded walking stick. I kept hearing their voices, too — Mamma's light, airy tone, Jeremy's boyish shout, and Papa's deep bass — until gradually they faded away and I could look into their empty rooms and hear nothing.

Chapter 4

Six weeks after the dreadful tragedy in Washington Brad, Laurel, and I sat in the drawing room of the Sixty-eighth Street house, heartsick and grief-stricken, listening to Mr. Cadell, Papa's lawyer, spell out the details of the shocking financial situation in which we found ourselves.

"Your father's will is explicit," he said seriously, glancing at each one of us in turn over the tops of his half glasses. "He left everything to your mother, to be hers for her lifetime, and upon her death to be divided equally among his four children. However, now that she is gone, and Jeremy Slade is deceased leaving no heirs, the estate will necessarily be divided amongst you three."

He paused for a moment or two and cleared his throat while he referred to the set of papers on the table in front of him.

"Unfortunately the estate is nowhere near as large as your father expected it to be. Mr. Slade apparently was ill advised by unscrupulous operators and took risks he should have shunned. He bought stocks on margin, and when they went down in value instead of going up, he mortgaged this house in order to raise money to cover his losses. He had always seemed to me to be far too astute a man to fall prey to the blandishments of the Wall Street gamblers. I was astonished when I realized the full extent of his debts."

He paused again, shaking his head either in sorrow or disbelief, maybe both.

"However," he continued slowly, "I shall be working with your father's executor, Mr. William Jerrold of the First Bank and Trust Company, and we'll see what we can salvage. At the moment it looks as if you'll each be lucky to realize as much as a hundred dollars a month on such securities as remain."

I thought at first that Laurel was going to faint at this announcement, but almost immediately she pulled herself together, and when I saw a certain calculating gleam come into her eyes I knew she was trying to decide which of the wealthy young men who had been courting her would make the most satisfactory husband. Brad, on the other hand, looked devastated.

"Is nothing at all to be realized on this house?" he asked in a hoarse voice. "It must be worth —"

"It is heavily mortgaged, Bradley," Mr. Cadell interrupted. "But of course if anything is realized on it or the furnishings — which, by the way, will be sold — after all debts are paid, that will be divided amongst the three of you."

"And Mamma's jewelry?" Laurel asked. "She had some quite valuable pieces."

"That, too, will be appraised and sold," the lawyer replied. "But you may keep your personal belongings, clothing and such. Right now you had better decide where you are going to live. Are there relatives with whom you could stay until you marry and settle down in homes of your own?"

When no one said anything, he prepared to leave. "Give it some thought," he said as he stood up, "and I will be in touch with you in a day or two."

"There's only Papa's brother . . ." I began when the door had closed on the lawyer.

"Who wants to live on a dairy farm in Vermont?" Laurel asked crossly. "No, I shall go visit Clara Radcliffe of the Philadelphia Radcliffes. She's invited me several times, but Mamma would never let me go. I can't imagine why."

"Don't do that, Laurel," Brad said quickly. "It's her brother, Desmond Radcliffe, who put her up to it. I saw him mooning over you when they were in New York in May. He's good-looking, but —"

"What's wrong with that?" my sister demanded. "They are Main Line Philadelphians with all kinds of money and houses at Bar Harbor and Palm Beach."

"What will you do, Brad?" I asked after we'd sat in silence for a few moments.

"Work hard for the rest of my life, I guess," he said resignedly. "And you, Caro, what will we do about you?"

"I'll manage," I said with a false show of confidence. "If I have a hundred dollars a month I can take a room someplace and live there while I go to the Normal College. That's free, you know — no tuition. Then I'll find a position teaching."

"How perfectly deadly!" Laurel exclaimed. "I wouldn't wish that on my worst enemy. Right now I'm going upstairs to write to Clara and tell her I'll be happy to accept her invitation. They're in Bar Harbor just now."

As I watched her go I wondered how many more times I would see her graceful figure hurrying up the wide marble staircase. She seemed made for such a setting as this house provided for such a short time. Not even a full year had elapsed since we moved in, and now it was all to be taken away from us.

"Perhaps," Brad said, turning to face me, "it would be a good idea for you and me to take an apartment, or rooms, Caro, until I pass the bar examination and get on my feet. I don't like the thought of you alone in a rooming house. I'll start looking for a place tomorrow afternoon; I'll be busy in the morning."

I was surprised and somewhat touched by his concern for me — or was he prompted by a sense of duty? At the same time I was a little dismayed that he simply assumed I'd agree to whatever arrangements he made. I merely nodded, however, and after glancing at the clock on the mantelpiece said I'd better go and look for Caesar.

The cook, Mrs. Ellis, our one remaining servant, had let the big cat out into the garden, where I found him sitting on the wall twitching his tail from side to side as he stared at the Prentice house. I sat down on one of the uncomfortable painted wrought iron chairs Mamma had grouped around a small ornamental fountain and was thinking over Brad's proposal when I saw Leland Prentice approach the wall and begin to stroke Caesar's head. I was surprised that the cat, usually so wary of strangers, permitted such familiarity.

"You two seem to be friends," I said, rising and making my way toward them. "Caesar generally flees at the sight of a stranger."

"Oh, Miss Slade!" Mr. Prentice looked startled. "I didn't see you among the shrubbery. Caesar and I have become great friends. Oh, I — I know I wrote to you, but please allow me to offer my condolences verbally. You must be frightfully upset over the deaths in your family," he said, reaching for my hand.

"Thank you," I replied, seeing the concern in his eyes. "I appreciated your letter. It all still seems unreal, I mean impossible that such a thing could happen to us. I still expect to see Mamma sitting in the drawing room pouring tea, or Papa in his favorite chair in the library, or Jeremy running up the stairs two at a time to get a book he left in his room."

"It may be a long time before you let go of those images," Leland Prentice said gently, "but after a while you'll learn to cherish them, and to smile when they come to mind."

We were quiet for a few minutes while he continued to rub the contented cat's head.

"The house will be sold," I said, looking up at my bedroom window, "and I will have to live in an apartment with my brother,

Bradley. Laurel, my sister, is going to visit friends for now. After that, I just don't know."

"Do you want to live with your brother?" he asked.

"I don't know that, either. I haven't been able to think it through. The lawyer was here this afternoon to tell us we won't have much money — oh, it's all so confusing."

"My aunt would like you to visit her in Newport, you know. She said she was writing to you. It might be a good idea, Miss Slade. Would you consider it? Be good for her, too, I think. The poor soul is just as lonely there as she is here."

At that point Caesar jumped down from the wall and ran to the door leading to the kitchen.

"Yes, I'll think about going to Newport, Mr. Prentice. If Laurel and Brad don't make too much fuss — but now, if you'll excuse me I'd better see to Caesar's supper. Sometimes I think the cook gives him too much food."

The letter from Miss Prentice inviting me to spend a month in Newport came two days later, and when I showed it to Laurel and

Brad at dinner that night they both urged me to go. I'd be out of the way, Laurel said, at least for a few weeks while the house was being sold. She made me feel as if I were a troublesome child who had to be shunted off to a relative while the rest of the family tended to important business, but I said nothing. Laurel had never been particularly careful about my feelings.

Brad was gentler: He said he thought a visit to Newport would be an experience to remember, and that he would make the travel arrangements for me.

"The thing to do is to take the Fall River Line. Elspeth told me about their newest boat, the *Priscilla*. She and her parents took it last year, and liked it immensely. I'll get you a stateroom — an outside one. They're not that expensive. You'll have dinner and a night's sleep, and be in Newport in the morning. Do it, Caro!

"I'll try to have an apartment lined up by the time you come back, someplace in the Sixties so you won't have to travel too far to the Normal College, but I don't even know yet what we'll be able to afford. God, it's all such a mess."

"Get Caro married to the old lady's nephew, Brad," Laurel said briskly. "Then she'll be off your hands."

I was too shocked to protest this outrageous suggestion, and glad when Brad told her roughly to shut up. It didn't bother her; she merely smiled and left the table, saying she had to decide which clothes to take to Bar Harbor.

"She's turned into the most self-centered, egotistical —" Brad muttered.

"She can't help it, Brad," I interrupted. "She's so beautiful that people fall all over themselves to please her, and she's come to expect it. She would have made a terrific queen of France, say for Louis the Fourteenth."

"Well, there are no kings around here," he growled. "She'll have to be satisfied with a robber baron or a railroad tycoon. Anyway, Caro, I don't believe we'll see much of her from now on, and maybe that's just as well. Hadn't you better write to Miss Prentice? You do want to go, don't you? I'll look after Caesar, I promise."

Miss Prentice's description of her "cottage" as unpretentious was, I thought, a serious understatement. The rambling, gray-shingled house with its numerous eaves and gables, almost totally screened from the road by tall trees and dense shrubbery, seemed to be making an effort to retire completely from the outer world. Not until one went through the wide, dimly lighted center hall to the veranda that stretched across the entire rear of the house and overlooked the water did any feeling of claustrophobia dissipate.

Then there was the coach house, also surrounded by overgrown shrubbery, situated a short distance away on the north end of the property. It was equipped, I learned later on, with sleeping quarters for the coachman and his helpers above the stables and the area where not one, but two coaches had been kept in readiness for use all summer long in years gone by. Empty now of the trappings and grandeur of the past, the building stood neglected, weathered and worn, a relic of Miss Prentice's girlhood.

The many rooms in the house itself — I counted nine bedrooms alone — although large, were darkened by trees and shrubbery crowding far too close to the house. Without exception they were furnished, or rather overfurnished, in the fashion of an earlier era, with so many tables, cabinets, armchairs, and screens strewn about that the overall picture was one of perpetual clutter.

Miss Prentice told me that she had kept

everything just as her mother left it, and when I looked around the gloomy dining room at the preponderance of china sets in the glass-enclosed cabinets and the heavy silver serving dishes on the massive black walnut sideboard I could easily believe that she had never rid herself of anything, however ugly and useless. There were times at meals when I felt oppressed by the heavy furniture surrounding us, feeling as if it all might suddenly move into the center of the room, spilling china, silver, and glass over the table and crushing us in the bargain.

I don't mean to give the impression that I was unhappy at Newport; I enjoyed the regimen, with breakfast at eight, lunch at one, tea at four, and dinner at eight. Miss Prentice had an excellent cook, and the food was invariably delicious, with things like eggs Benedict or crabmeat salad for lunch and duck à l'orange for dinner. It did, however, take me a while to become accustomed to living in a house that was more like a museum than a home. My eyes longed for Mamma's bright colors, her airy drawing room with its comfortable lamplight, and the cheerful, sunny windows of her sitting room. No, I was not unhappy, although I did not see much of Newport itself, since Miss Prentice did not go out at all except to sit on the veranda or to walk on the long stretch of sand in front of the house. Without a cane, too.

Although there wasn't very much to do, and I was a bit lonely at times, I was never bored. There was a small but well-stocked library across the hall from the drawing room that provided me with all the reading material I could possibly want, and then there was the garden. Miss Prentice was a devoted gardener, and before long I was as interested in the procession of the blossoms as she was. On fine mornings, after the dew was off the grass, we'd spend an hour or two among the precisely laid out flower beds, all of which were sheltered from the sea breezes by a six-foot-high stone wall. Of course Miss Prentice had a gardener, Anton, to do the heavy work, but she was not above kneeling down on a little mat to separate the crowded marigolds or to plant some late asters Anton had found in a nursery.

"Those lilies are suffocating the poppies in front of them, Caroline. Overbearing they are, like some people. Remind me to tell Anton to cut them back, or better still, to take them out. I never did like lillies — they smell of death and funerals. The phlox is lovely, though, so delicate and fragrant. Doesn't it look spectacular there up against the broken column?"

"Yes, it does," I agreed. "But tell me — there must be a story about that column."

"Oh, yes indeed, my dear, there is," she said with a smile. "Years ago, before I was born, my parents traveled to Greece. It must have been a particularly happy trip because Father loved to talk about it. And he had insisted on bringing home a memento of the trip. He told us later that marbles were all the rage at the time — everyone was buying them — but since he couldn't find a statue that suited him, probably because of their nudity, he settled on that column and had it shipped here. I can see why he liked it. Corinthian, he said it was. See, Caroline, how beautifully the leaves are carved! And the proportions are so good, although you can't judge them now. The height was just eight feet, and the diameter eighteen inches. Perfect!

"Well, he had it mounted on a pedestal, and ordered a special planting around the base. Everything was fine for a number of years, and then one September a terrible storm came up and toppled it over so that it broke. It still lies where it fell, as you see it, with part of it on the ground, and the part with the leaves leaning at an angle against it.

"I was fifteen or sixteen at the time, and I still remember how Father stood looking at it for a while before shaking his head and saying, 'Well, girls, I understand that in England it was once fashionable — maybe it still is — to have a ruin of some sort on your property, and now with no effort on our part we have a ruin of our own!' "

"Did he never want to have the column mended?" I asked.

"No, he simply ordered different plantings around it, and sometimes he'd come out and sit on the horizontal part, rubbing his fingers across the marble. Yes, he must have had happy memories of that trip to Greece. Of course I would never think of changing anything."

We stood quietly for a few minutes in that peaceful spot, and when I saw how the sunlight warmed the ancient stone of the broken column I thought I could understand why Mr. Prentice wanted it left where it fell — something like the end of the golden age of Greece itself.

"Oh, dear," I heard Miss Prentice say. "I almost forgot: The rhubarb at the edge of the kitchen garden is past its prime. It's only tasty when it's young. And the leaves, you know, are poisonous. I have heard that as far back as the fifteenth century the Medicis and the Borgias and the rest of those people used to grind the leaves up into a powder and slip it into the wine of courtiers they mistrusted. Such secrets they had —"

She stopped suddenly, turned away from me, and began to clip the dead blooms from a rose bush. I wondered about that. It wasn't like her to leave a sentence unfinished, to leave the thought in midair.

Besides her garden, Miss Prentice had a genuine interest in conchology. She'd made a study of it quite on her own, and as we strolled along the edge of the water, picking up an occasional shell, she was able to spin stories, true or fanciful, about their whorls and ridges. She really did love to talk; at mealtimes, especially at tea and dinner, she liked to reminisce about her girlhood summers, the archery tournaments, the dancing on the grass at meetings of the Coaching Club, and the formal banquets.

"And oh, the dresses, my dear! We almost always wore white in those days, long flowing skirts and enormous floppy hats, some of them outrageously decorated with feathers and ribbons. No one, or very few, ever dared to be different; we were all conditioned, you might say, to what society decreed. I sometimes wonder if that didn't make us too inhibited. . . ."

For a few moments she looked so wistful that I wondered if there hadn't been someone in her past, a suitor deemed unworthy by her parents, perhaps? I was thinking, too, of Laurel, free now that Papa was dead to make her own choice, when the doorbell rang, and a moment later the maid came in to say that Mr. Leland had just arrived.

"Leland! My dear boy!" Miss Prentice exclaimed as he came into the drawing room where we were finishing our tea. "What a surprise! You haven't been here since —"

"Since I was a boy, Aunt," he said with a laugh. "I know, I know. It's never been my favorite place, but New York has been a veritable oven for the past week, and I craved some cool sea breezes."

"Well of course I am delighted, dear. Sit down and have some tea with us."

Although her manner was warm and welcoming, I thought she looked somewhat puzzled, and when she picked up the little bell to ring for fresh tea I noticed that her hand trembled slightly. She recovered quickly, however, from whatever was troubling her and bombarded Leland with questions about the condition of her household in the city.

Was her canary properly looked after? Had Gordon seen that the rugs were taken up and sent out to be cleaned, and what about the new awnings she'd ordered for the windows facing south? Had they arrived?

"Yes to everything, Aunt," Leland answered. "All has been done as you requested. The awnings are a great success. Now I can leave my bedroom windows wide open, even in a downpour."

"Good," she said, smiling over at him. "Would you like another cup, dear?"

"No, thank you. What I'd really like would be to stretch my legs on the beach. How about you, Aunt Henrietta? A little walk, a little talk?"

"I believe not today, Leland. I have some things to attend to. Caroline, wouldn't you . . . ?"

"Yes, Caroline," Leland said quickly, standing up and holding his hand out to me. "Come along and keep me company. Keep me from brooding over my wasted youth."

"Oh, Leland! Why do you talk such nonsense?" Miss Prentice asked, shaking her finger at him. "Don't pay any attention to him, my dear. His youth was no more wasted than yours or mine. Now off with you. I have things to do before dinner."

"She simply refuses to face up to the truth of the matter: that I am indeed a lazy, indolent ne'r-do-well who refuses to read law, study finance, or follow some other worthy career," he said gloomily as we stepped off the veranda and onto the sand.

"What *do* you do, Leland?" I asked. "You cannot be completely idle."

"Some days I am. Especially when the writing isn't going well."

As we walked, far more briskly than I had with Miss Prentice, I learned that he'd had three short novels published, all dealing with the lives of the early settlers in New England, and that he was at present working on a book about witchcraft in Salem.

"It's a good thing I don't have to support myself on my royalties, Caroline," he said ruefully, kicking a stone out of his way. "I'd never be able to live on the proceeds of my literary output. Writing doesn't pay very well, at least mine doesn't. Maybe someday, though. . . ."

I forget the rest of that afternoon's conversation, but I do remember that it was the only occasion on which I was alone with Leland in Newport for any length of time.

He may have wanted a few hours alone, perhaps to think about his book, because twice he excused himself immediately after lunch and went off by himself. I have no idea where he went, but Miss Prentice may have known, because she merely nodded when he left the room.

Part II

Leland

Chapter 5

I like coming over here to the old coach house, climbing up to the room I so often occupied as a boy, and stretching out on the narrow cot I slept on many a hot night. It's peaceful here, with no one to interrupt or disturb my thoughts. I can review my past life — such as it has been — at my leisure and try to figure out why it has been so different from the lives of other men.

Well, to begin:

I always thought I was educated at home with tutors in the various disciplines, English, Latin, French, mathematics, and history, because that was how boys in wealthy families were brought up. Maybe some of them were, but since I never went to school I had no opportunity to make friends of my own age, and by the time I realized that my situation was unusual, it was too late to try to remedy it.

I place the blame for my closely guarded, restricted life solely on my Aunt Henrietta's shoulders. She hand-picked my tutors, paid them well, and did not hesitate to dismiss any she suspected of giving me ideas that would lead to independent thought on my part.

She made one mistake, though: Like most women in her walk of life, she was not a reader. She had no idea of the extent of worldly knowledge I gained from the volumes I found in the library across the hall from the dining room, books probably purchased by her father when he was furnishing the house for her. That library, and the one here at Corinth, where we spent so many dreadful summers, were the saving of me.

When I reached what my aunt called "man's estate" she relinquished her control of me, and depended completely on Gordon for reports of my interests and activities. I think she was afraid I'd rebel and leave her (by that time I was independently wealthy) if she continued to treat me like a child who needed constant supervision. While I enjoyed the *idea* of freedom, I soon realized that I'd been so sheltered, almost to the point of being a recluse, that when the bonds were loosened I was not prepared to enjoy the *reality* of being my own master. For example, at first I thought I'd dine out at some of the finest restaurants in the city, and in one way or another meet and become friends with interesting people. After a few solitary dinners, however, in places like Delmonico's and the Astor Hotel and the Hoffman House, where no one paid the slightest attention to me, I gave up. Or rather, I was ready to give up and retreat into my old life when I met Marcella.

I came out of the Metropolitan Museum one afternoon — I'd been to a special exhibition of French paintings — and was walking down Fifth Avenue on the park side when I noticed that a young woman just ahead of me had dropped one of her gloves. Naturally I picked it up, and when I returned it to her she looked at me in astonishment.

"Oh," she gasped, "aren't you Dickie Gillespie?"

"No," I answered, "I am sorry to say I'm not. My name is Leland Prentice."

"You look so much like him. Prentice, you say? Where have I heard that name? It sounds familiar, somehow."

I couldn't take my eyes from her face. Even when she frowned in an effort to remember where she'd heard my name she looked absolutely beautiful. Softly curling blond hair, only partly visible under an elaborate velvet bonnet, framed a face I thought men would die for. How can I describe her? High cheek-bones, creamy skin, a straight little nose, and delicate pink lips — no, no such description could possibly do her justice. I was lost. In the few minutes we stood looking at each other I fell hopelessly and completely in love for the first time.

Everything the poets say about love at first sight is true. I know that. I was deliriously happy in the days that followed our meeting, and Marcella (how I adored that name!) received the attentions I paid — flowers, trips to the theaters, dinners at fancy restaurants — with what seemed to be great pleasure. And so it went, all through the late winter and spring of that year. I'd never been so happy in my life, and I do not believe I've ever been that happy again.

All went well, better than well, until the night she came to have dinner with us in Sixty-ninth Street. I was anxious to have Aunt Henrietta meet her so that when I told her I intended to marry Marcella it would not be a complete surprise, but something, I'm not quite sure what it was, went wrong, very wrong at that little dinner party.

Marcella looked lovelier than ever that evening in a gold-colored gown that shimmered in the light cast by the tall candles set in the heavy silver candelabra. I sat across the table from her, and when she smiled and nodded at some remark of mine I could see her expressive brown eyes register instant understanding and interest.

I remember that Gordon was removing the fish plates and that we were telling my aunt about a play we'd seen a few nights before when I suddenly lost the thread of the conversation. The next thing I knew I was sitting in the butler's pantry with Gordon, who was telling me that everything was all right, that I'd just had a bit of a spell.

"The excitement of the dinner party, Mr. Leland," he said. "That's all it was. You're all right now."

I went back into the dining room ready to apologize to Marcella and to assure her that I was perfectly well only to find her place empty. My aunt was complacently eating her dessert.

"She was frightened, Leland," Aunt Henrietta said, smiling quietly as if nothing out of the ordinary had happened. "Apparently she is one of those people who cannot stand the sight of even a momentary indisposition. She flew out of here without so much as a hurried adieu."

I was crestfallen, and even more disheartened the following day when I called at Marcella's house — she lived with her brother

and his family on Seventy-third Street —
only to be told that she was not at home. For
the next several days I tried in vain to see
her, but my efforts were of no avail, and not
one of the many letters I wrote to her was
answered.

That was the end of my first love affair —
oh, there were two or three others later on,
all of them with pretty, blond, slender young
women whom I met by chance. I won't go
into that except to say that although I never
invited any of them for dinner, each one put
an end to our relationship rather abruptly for
no reason that I could fathom.

About those "spells": I have no idea what
causes them (I still have them from time to
time), and I can never remember what went
on while I was having one. Before I met
Marcella I hadn't had one for months,
which prompted Gordon to say that I had
probably outgrown them. Evidently I hadn't,
but I've found that a drink or two makes me
forget about them and feel better.

The spells were the reason Aunt Henrietta
said I shouldn't marry. At least that's what
she said when I forced her to talk about
them, but I think it's quite possible that she
just didn't want to be left alone. I did feel
sorry for the old lady who'd been so good to
me (sorry for myself, too), and for a few years

I devoted myself to her and to my writing. I was elated at the mild success of my three novels and am determined to make my study of witchcraft in Salem a serious work that will benefit scholars in years to come.

I hope I do not become distracted, but I am afraid I will. Caroline is a sweet, pleasant girl, but her sister is an absolute beauty — at least that is my opinion from the few glimpses I've had of her. I must meet her — I must. . . .

Part III

Caroline

Chapter 6

After that one walk I had with Leland either Miss Prentice accompanied us or else I made some excuse to stay home, thinking they might have private matters to discuss. They did seem to have plenty to talk about: On several occasions after I had gone up to bed they remained in the drawing room, and I didn't imagine that they sat there in silence.

Indeed, they did not: Late one night toward the end of Leland's week with us I was restless, and thinking a drink of warm milk would help me sleep I went down to the kitchen for it. As I passed the still closed drawing room door I paused, surprised to hear Miss Prentice's usually soft voice raised, saying:

"Leland! Don't be silly! We've been over this so many times."

"I know, Aunt, but I can't help it. She's so beautiful! I've seen her —"

I hurried on down the passage, thinking it

would be better for me, once I had the milk, to return to my room by means of the back stairs than to risk passing the drawing room door a second time.

Since the only light in the kitchen came from a gas fixture near the stove, the greater part of that large room lay in deep shadows, and I suddenly felt uneasy. I was about to go back upstairs empty-handed when the full moon, which must have been obscured by a cloud until then, shone in through the window over the sink, making the place more cheerful.

I was standing near the stove, waiting for the milk to heat (and half wishing I'd never bothered to come down for it) when I heard a door slam. A moment later Leland burst into the kitchen and without pausing for a second rushed across the room and out the back door into the moonlit night. I did not think he saw me.

The next morning when Miss Prentice, looking paler than usual, appeared at the breakfast table she told me that Leland had left at dawn to return to the city to attend to some important business matters. Her tone was such that I didn't dare ask any questions.

Chapter 7

"I don't know why Leland doesn't use his common sense," Miss Prentice said, more to herself than to me as we walked along the beach at the water's edge a few days later. "He's twenty-eight years old, and certainly should have some by this time. He knows he can never marry, and yet he goes on falling in love with one beautiful girl after another, and then . . ."

"But why can't he marry, Miss Prentice?" I asked after a moment or two. "He told me he has a private income, so he could easily support a wife and family."

"Oh, money is not the problem, Caroline. It's his health. Doctors have warned us."

"I saw that he limped slightly, but really it is hardly noticeable. I can't see that that should be a problem."

"Oh, he broke his leg when he was a child. He fell out of a tree; we think the bone was not set properly. He had a terrible bump on his head, too. No, that has nothing to do with it, although, come to think of it — oh, enough of that. Look, look right there next to your left foot! That's a moon shell, *Lunetia heros*. I don't see many of them. And the little one next to it is a periwinkle, *Littorina littorea*. Aren't they fascinating? Look at the colors! I'll take them home to compare with the ones I have."

With further thought of Leland banished by her delight in the shells, Miss Prentice looked happier than she had since her nephew left. It would be cruel, I thought, watching her slip the two small shells into the little mesh bag she carried on our walks, to return to the subject of his illness, but I was indeed puzzled by her remarks concerning his health. By her own admission the broken leg and bump on the head he had sustained had nothing to do with his not being able to marry. What was it, then? Was that the secret I suspected her of hiding when she was speaking of the Borgias and broke off in midsentence? And why had Leland left Corinth so abruptly the morning after I saw him dash through the kitchen and out into the night? Also, if he "kept falling in love with one beautiful girl after another," wouldn't you think he'd be married by now? And what had the doctors warned them about?

In the end I concluded that whatever had happened to Leland to make him ineligible for marriage did not concern me, and that I had better not ask any more questions.

Leland's name was not mentioned again during the rest of my stay in Newport, but he was never out of my thoughts for long. I could not go into the kitchen for a cookie or a piece of fruit without recalling that desperate figure heading for the back door. One way or another he had spoiled the peaceful, pleasant atmosphere of the place, and I was almost relieved when the time came for me to leave.

Miss Prentice seemed genuinely sorry to see me go.

"You've been such a comfort to me, Caroline," she said the night before I left. "I wish you could stay until the summer is over. Next year you must plan on a longer visit. I shall be counting on it, my dear."

Once back in New York I had little time to allow my thoughts to dwell on either of the Prentices. The mansion in which we'd lived for such a short time, now stripped of everything of value, had taken on the forlorn look that houses have when people are preparing to move out, and I was glad that Mamma could not see it. It would have broken her heart.

"Good news, Caro," Brad said happily as soon as I stepped into the nearly empty drawing room. "We don't need to rent an apartment after all. I didn't know — no one seemed to know, and the lawyers forgot to mention it — we still own the Harrison Street house! I thought Papa had sold it, but it turns out that he just rented it to the Conklins, rented it furnished, and they're moving out next month. It's ours!"

"How on earth —"

"The Conklins were all set to buy it, but at the last minute changed their minds and asked if they could rent instead. Papa had already bought this place, and evidently thought it easier to let them have it than to put it on the market again. Anyway, Caro, we can live there rent free!"

"What did Laurel say?"

"She doesn't know yet. She's off somewhere or other. We'll have to carry on here for a month longer. When does your school start?"

"Early in September, I think. I'll have to look."

"We'll probably still be here then. Think you can put up with all this emptiness for a while? Almost everything seems to be gone except our clothes and our beds and Mrs. Ellis. I can't imagine why she stays, we pay her so little."

"Maybe she has no other place to go."

"Anyway," Brad said after a moment or two, "it's a good thing it's still warm weather and we don't have to heat the place."

Warm weather or not, the house seemed cold, and I found myself spending more and more time in the neglected garden with my books than I spent indoors. I was there one afternoon reading up on the wars between Athens and Sparta, concentrating on the passages Jeremy had underlined, when Leland Prentice called to me from his side of the wall. He looked perfectly calm, not at all like the distraught figure I had seen dash through the kitchen in Newport. Indeed, he was unusually cheerful. He'd just had a meeting with his editor, he said, who had been most encouraging about his novel on witchcraft.

"You'll never know, Caroline, what it means to hear that what you've written is good!" he exclaimed. "I was so discouraged for a while — I was about to give up on the whole thing. That's the real reason I went to Newport, to get away from it for a while, and to try to pull my thoughts together."

He was more animated than I had ever seen him, talking excitedly about the research he'd done recently and the plans he had for expanding the chapter on devil worship.

"Hawthorne did it so well, you know," he said, "that I sometimes wonder if I have a nerve to attempt a story . . ."

He broke off suddenly and stared vacantly over my head. I turned to see what had attracted his attention, or rather what had distracted him, but could see nothing out of the ordinary.

"Oh, yes," he said quietly when I looked back at him. "Oh, yes, it's quite a problem. I must get on with it now." And with no further word he hurried away, leaving me to wonder at his sudden change of mood.

I tried to make some sense out of the information I had: the reason he had just given for going to Newport, the angry words I had overheard there, what Miss Prentice had told me about him, and Leland's flight, first out into the night and then back to the city. It must all be connected, I thought, but how? I was still mulling over the strange series of events when Brad called to me, crossly, I thought, to come into the house.

Laurel, home between visits and looking quite satisfied with herself, was with him in the small sitting room. Brad looked anything but satisfied as he thrust a sheaf of papers into my hands.

"Read this and weep, Caro," he said brusquely. "Those executors don't know what they're doing! After telling us the Harrison Street house was ours they've gone and sold it to the Conklins, saying it was part of the estate and that the money was needed to help cover some damn debts Papa ran up. Now we'll *have* to rent a place, and they want us out of here as soon as possible. Of all the incompetent fools."

"Really, Brad," Laurel said impatiently. "The sooner you're out of this mausoleum the better. Can't you see that?"

"What about you, Laurel?" I asked. "Shall we take a flat large enough for the three of us?"

"No need for that, my dear," she said airily. "The senior Radcliffes have invited me to go to Europe with them. They say I'll be company for Clara, but I know that they think I'll attract men to pay court to her. Anyway, with any luck I'll come back married to Clara's brother — I'll be Mrs. Desmond Radcliffe. We're sailing on the *Maure-tania* in October, and in the meantime I'm going to visit the Whittakers on Long Island — polo, you know. From there I'll go on to the Radcliffes in Philadelphia. I just stopped in here to pick up a few things. Don't look so disapproving, you two. I'll have the life I've always wanted, luxury, money, every-thing."

"Well," Brad said after a pause, "I'll look for a two-bedroom flat then."

When Laurel went off in a taxi the next morning, Brad was out, so I was the only one to wish her bon voyage and wave good-bye to her. Mrs. Ellis couldn't be bothered; Laurel had never paid any attention to her, she said. As the taxi turned into Fifth Ave-nue and disappeared downtown and I was wondering when I'd see my sister again, if ever, I noticed Leland Prentice standing at the corner, staring fixedly after the cab. When he turned and noticed me he waved off-handedly and walked quickly toward Sixty-ninth Street.

Confident that Brad would find a place to live, I spent the rest of the day packing clothes, books (mine and Jeremy's), and whatever else I thought I'd need. By four o'clock I was heartily sick of deciding what was essential and what was not, and glad when Mrs. Ellis called up to me that she was making iced tea. I knew that she was sad about leaving what she called "such a grand house," but I was surprised when she told me that she'd come with Brad and me if we could find room for her.

"But we won't be able to pay you very much," I protested.

"It'll be a roof over my head," she said, "and whatever you can pay, even a little, will be all right for now."

"Of course we'd love to have you, Mrs. Ellis —"

"See what Mr. Brad says," she interrupted. "He's the boss now."

I took my glass of tea out into the garden and sat where a light breeze carried the scent of Leland's flowers toward me and reminded me of Miss Prentice's garden in Newport. Strange, I thought, remembering the hours I spent with her among the blossoms there, that she pays no attention to these. Perhaps it's just that she doesn't want to interfere with Leland's plantings. He didn't come out that day, and after a while the place seemed so unbearably lonely that I went back indoors to wait for Brad.

Chapter 8

I don't know what we would have done if Miss Prentice had not returned to the city when she did. The apartments, or flats, that Brad took me to see were either beyond our means or miserable tenement-like rooms with a bath that had to be shared with neighbors. There seemed to be nothing in between these two extremes, and we trudged back to our nearly empty mansion, tired and discouraged, each day during the week following Laurel's departure.

To make matters worse, men came and boarded up the windows facing the street, to prevent vandalism, they said. I was reminded of a play I once read about some old Spanish queen who was condemned to live out her days in a boarded-up palazzo. I can't remember what her crime was, but I couldn't put her out of my mind. Naturally we gravitated to the back of the house and the garden, but we probably weren't any happier than that old queen was.

The boarding up of the windows was too much for Mrs. Ellis. First she said it was like being in a prison, and then she complained that she felt as if she were living in a haunted house.

"I hear all them rattlings and creakings in the night," she said, "and you know what they mean — ghosts!"

We tried to cnvince her that it was only the wind, but to no avail.

"No, Miss Caroline, I ain't stayin'," she said. "There's somethin' evil here now. I can feel it. You and Mr. Brad had best move out, too. I'll go to my sister. She has a couch in the parlor where I can sleep until I find another place. I've written her address down on the paper in the kitchen in case you want me sometime. Oh, an' I've left a cold supper for you, and Caesar's food is ready. I haven't seen that cat all day, though. I think he went off when the hammering began."

"Maybe we'd better settle for a rooming house," Brad said as we approached the house the following afternoon after another fruitless search. "It won't be elegant, but at least we can afford two rooms until something better shows up. Hello, who's that?"

91

Leland Prentice had been about to start up our front steps when he saw us coming. He turned, and after I introduced him to Brad he held out an envelope addressed to me in Miss Prentice's distinctive hand.

"My aunt arrived home yesterday, Caroline," he said, "and desires to see you both. Please come for tea tomorrow; here is her written invitation. She's very upset about what's going on, and worried about you. Oh, and if your sister is at home of course she is included in the invitation."

I heard the eagerness in his voice when he said "your sister," and I think it was then that I realized the "beautiful girl" he said he had seen, the one he mentioned that night in Newport, was Laurel. And he'd been watching her drive off in the taxi that morning.

Brad and I did walk around the block to the Prentice house the next afternoon to what my brother later said turned out to be, outside of *Alice in Wonderland*, the most unusual tea party anyone ever attended.

When we were shown into the sitting room Leland turned from where he'd been standing at the window and greeted us pleasantly.

I wondered if he wasn't disappointed that there were just the two of us. Miss Prentice sat not in her usual wing chair, but behind the beautiful Louis Quinze desk on the far side of the room. She stood up to welcome us, and as I introduced her to Brad I could see that she was looking him over carefully, as if to see if he were someone she'd care to know. (Brad said later he'd felt as if he'd been put under a microscope.)

"I'll come right to the point," she said when tea, sandwiches, and the ever-present madeleines had been served. "Leland has informed me of your predicament, and I am shocked at the crass treatment you have received from the trustees or executors or whatever they are of your father's will. Tell me, Mr. Slade, where do you intend to live?"

"Probably in a rooming house," Brad replied, "at least until we can find something suitable that we can afford."

"Oh dear me, no, no, not a rooming house."

"We really don't have a choice, Miss Prentice," I said, surprised at the agitation and concern in her voice.

"Yes, yes you do, my dear Caroline," she said more calmly. "I see no reason why you both should not move in here."

"Here?" I gasped. "But —"

"Just a moment, please. There are three empty bedrooms, two of them connected by a sitting room, up on the third floor. They have never, in all the years, been used, and it has always been my wish to see them occupied, either by children, young people, or almost anyone. This house needs some new life brought into it."

Brad looked as stunned as I felt; we simply stared at each other without speaking for a few moments while Leland and Miss Prentice continued to watch us.

"We couldn't pay —" Brad said finally.

"Nor need you," she interrupted. "You will be my honored guests. I am very fond of Caroline, you know. She was a wonderful guest in Newport during the summer. You would both be able to come and go as you pleased, and I'm sure the food here will be better for you than what you'd have in a rooming house. But most important of all, you'd be making an old lady feel that at long last she is doing something for someone other than herself."

She paused and looked at us expectantly.

"You are most kind, Miss Prentice," Brad said slowly, "but I am afraid we cannot —"

"Please do not decide in a hurry, young man," she interrupted. "Perhaps you would like to confer with your sister?"

"No, that won't be necessary, Miss Prentice. I was about to say that we cannot accept your kind offer on anything like a permanent basis, but if you would put us up until we find suitable lodgings we'd be most grateful. You see, our house has been practically stripped bare; even our cook has left."

"Then you must certainly have dinner here tonight," she said briskly. "Go home now and pack just what you need immediately, and then tomorrow I'll send Gordon over with you to help with the rest of your things."

Leland, who had been silent during this entire conversation, smiled at me and said that Caesar could live in the kitchen and prowl in his garden instead of in ours.

"Oh, he may come back now that it's quiet again," he said when I told him of Caesar's departure. "Cats often do return after a few days."

Caesar never did come back, though, and it was a long time before I found a replacement for him.

Miss Prentice had her way, and in no time

at all Brad and I were comfortably, very comfortably, established on her beautifully furnished third floor, marveling at our good fortune. Brad spent his days either looking for an apartment or studying for the bar examination, and I began my classes at the Normal College.

I rather liked it there, in spite of all the rules and regulations. We had to form in line for everything, going to the morning assembly in the large auditorium or from one classroom to another, and of course while waiting to get into the lunchroom, where only quiet conversation was allowed. No talking was permitted in the halls at all. The dress code was simple: a plain white shirt-waist tucked into a dark, ankle-length skirt, and no jewelry or ornamentation of any kind. Our jackets and hats were to be hung neatly on assigned pegs in the cloakroom. It really wasn't so bad, but neither was it anything like what I had been accustomed to.

The daily assembly periods bored me to distraction. We were told that the recitation of a number of lines of reputable prose or poetry would develop our memories and give us the confidence we needed to stand up and speak in front of a group. The recitations were supposed to be completely voluntary, but the girl who sat next to me in geometry class said that the professors, who sat in a formidable row on the platform, kept a record of which students volunteered and which sat glued to their seats.

The selections chosen for recitation varied tremendously. On a typical morning the program might start with a four-line quotation from one of Bacon's essays (nervously and hurriedly delivered), followed by what seemed like yards of verse from Tennyson's *Idylls of the King* (that girl must have had a terrific memory), and end with someone racing through Milton's sonnet "On His Blindness" at top speed.

I was not anxious to stand up and "say my piece," but after talking it over with Miss Prentice I decided I'd better do it and have it over with. After much deliberation we settled on Portia's speech on the quality of mercy from *The Merchant of Venice*, and every afternoon for a week she rehearsed me in it. I think she enjoyed suggesting a certain emphasis here, a pause there, and I am sure she loved reminiscing about how her mother used to quote the lines years ago.

"I wish you could have heard her, Caroline," Miss Prentice said. "I remember so well how she'd say, 'If the world understood how important mercy is, my daughter, it would be a far better place.' And, my dear,

I never forgot that. I truly believe that mercy is an attribute of God himself."

"I'm not at all surprised," she said when I told her that there had been a spontaneous round of applause when I sat down after reciting those wonderful lines. "You have a lovely voice, my dear, and of course your diction is faultless."

I didn't tell her, but personally I thought the whole thing was a waste of time.

Another waste of time as far as I was concerned was the fifteen-minute period devoted to calisthenics each day. God alone knows what good it did us to walk slowly around the gymnasium waving our arms (supposedly gracefully) and swaying slightly in time to music. We each held a strong elastic band with two wooden handles in our hands and, following the directions of the instructor, raised it over our heads, stretched it from side to side, and then lowered it from chin to waist.

Ridiculous, I thought as I left the gymnasium and made my way to the history classroom. My reaction must have been more evident than I meant it to be, because Mr. Rambush, our history professor, who had spent a few minutes observing our antics, smiled at me and said quietly: "I quite agree with you, Miss Slade."

I rather liked him for that.

When I described our so-called calisthenics to Miss Prentice that afternoon she laughed and shook her head.

"An hour spent in the garden, Caroline, stooping, bending, and digging would be far more beneficial, but since there are no gardens in the Normal College I guess they just have to make do."

Since I had plenty of time to devote to my studies in the late afternoons and evenings, I kept well up in them, but some of my classmates worked as waitresses or maids or shopgirls after school was over for the day. It couldn't have been easy for them. Molly Krazak, a pretty young woman with whom I had several classes, told me that her father owned a florist shop on Third Avenue, and that she had to help out there in the afternoons and on Saturdays.

"It's not hard work, Caroline," she said. "I'm not like poor Angie Basso, who has to wash dishes in her uncle's restaurant. All the same, there are days when I'd give anything to be able to go right home from school, put my feet up, and get the German verbs into my head before my eyes start to close."

I made it a practice to be in bed by ten o'clock at the latest, and usually slept soundly until about seven in the morning. On two separate occasions, however, I was awakened during the night by some unidentifiable noise. The first time it happened I thought it might have been the slamming of a door, and since a strong breeze was blowing in through my open bedroom windows I dismissed it as such. The second time, though, and this was toward the end of September, I definitely heard a loud shout, and then a groan, as if someone were in pain. Without stopping to put on my robe I rushed into the hall outside my room and leaned over the banister of the stairs leading down to the second floor.

At first I could see nothing in the dimly lighted passage below me, but a moment or two later Gordon appeared, supporting, almost carrying, Leland in his arms. I couldn't see Leland's face since his head was hanging down, but I noticed that his feet were dragging and that his arms hung limply. Both men were in their nightclothes, and I thought I heard Gordon speak soothingly to the younger man before they disappeared into one of the bedrooms.

Had Leland had a bad dream? I wondered. A nightmare? Or had he been walking in his sleep? I remembered that Jeremy used to wander about in his sleep until someone led him back to his bed, but that was when he was a little boy. . . .

I went quietly back to my room, and for the first time since I'd been in the Prentice house I locked my door.

Chapter 9

I think it was because I was afraid of alarming Miss Prentice that I didn't mention to her or to anyone else what I had seen that night. I could have told Brad, I suppose, but he was so involved in preparations for his examination that I hesitated to bother him. In any case, there were no further nighttime incidents, and in mid-October my brother passed the bar exam the first time he took it, and became an associate at Lewis, Crouch, and Fisk. Miss Prentice was as delighted as he was, and ordered an especially festive dinner to celebrate.

Brad's new salary made it possible for us to rent a furnished floor-through apartment in a brownstone house on Lexington Avenue near Sixty-fifth Street, which we had seen before but deemed too expensive at the time. Since it consisted of only four rooms (parlor, two bedrooms, kitchen, and bath), it seemed tiny, almost lilliputian in comparison to what we'd been used to in the Sixty-eighth Street house, but like a mansion when we remembered some of the hovels we'd looked at.

Miss Prentice was loath to see us go, but she was a reasonable woman, and understood that we could not in conscience continue to "sponge" (Brad's word) on her forever.

"We shall certainly miss you, my dear, won't we, Leland?" she remarked one afternoon the week before we were to move when the three of us were having tea. "This house will seem empty again."

"We won't be far away," I said. "Sixty-fifth Street is only four blocks south and Lexington is three blocks east, an easy walk, so I'll be able to stop in whenever you like, and —"

I never finished that sentence, for just then Gordon knocked to announce that my sister had arrived with her luggage.

I had to give Laurel credit; she was not in that drawing room for more than ten minutes before she had Leland almost at her feet. Miss Prentice, I thought, looked startled.

"I had such a time finding you, Caro," she said after the introductions had been made.

103

"I couldn't imagine where you and Brad were when I saw the house all boarded up, so I went to Mr. Cadell's office — I'd been there once with Papa — and he enlightened me. How very good of Miss Prentice to take you in!"

"Perhaps you will join us, Miss Slade," Leland said after glancing at his aunt. "There's room, isn't there, Aunt?"

"Yes, of course," Miss Prentice said in a noncommittal way. She'd been watching Leland, and I do not think she liked what she saw.

"And," Leland went on eagerly, "since Caroline and Brad are leaving us in a few days, there'll be even more room. Miss Slade could have the entire third floor, couldn't she?"

"Oh, where are you going?" Laurel asked, making no effort to hide the surprise and annoyance in her voice, or the disapproval in her expression when I described the apartment.

"Wouldn't you rather stay here?" she asked.

"Laurel! We can't impose on Miss Prentice indefinitely!"

"You've never imposed on me, my dear," Miss Prentice said quietly, giving Laurel a searching look. "On the contrary, you've been delightful company."

"Well, maybe Miss Slade will stay, Aunt," Leland said, smiling at Laurel.

"I'd really like to, at least until —"

"It's settled then!" Leland exclaimed. "There! You'll have one of the Slades for company, Aunt."

Miss Prentice made no reply, but somehow the matter was settled, and when Brad and I moved over to Lexington Avenue Laurel did have the third floor to herself.

The night before we left she came into my room and, after closing the door and making herself comfortable on the chaise longue, said she had to talk to me.

"I thought you were going to Europe with the Radcliffes," I said. "What happened to change your plans?"

"Oh, everything! And it all went wrong! But none of it was my fault. Yes, I was supposed to go to Europe, but then — oh . . ." She began to cry.

"Give me a handkerchief, Caro, please. I'll be all right in a minute."

She took her time coming to the point, but even though I was tired and anxious to get to bed I decided it would be unwise to try to hurry her.

"You've no idea how well the Radcliffes live, Caro," she said. "Oh, such luxury!

Plenty of servants, maids and valets and all — you never have to lift a finger in that house. Did I say house? It's more like a palace. I've never seen so many rooms, and they're all furnished in impeccable taste. They even have a ballroom! There was a grand party one night. Thank heavens Mamma had bought me that gold satin dress. I really was the star of the evening, or as Desmond's father whispered to me, the belle of the ball.

"We danced and danced, and then at midnight a wonderful supper was served. Such delicacies! All kinds of fish, crab, lobster, shrimp, creamed oysters — I passed them up — and then pheasant and beef and imported ham, all beautifully presented. And they had a huge ice carving of two swans for a centerpiece. I've never seen anything like it."

She leaned back on the chaise and closed her eyes for a moment or two, apparently lost in the memory of the gala evening.

"You'd have loved the conservatory, Caro," she said with a smile. "I loved going in there. The fragrance of the flowers was marvelous, and I could ask the gardener for a camelia or an orchid or whatever I wanted to pin in my hair or on my dress. I was really having a wonderful time. In the morning we'd ride, and after lunch it was the custom to rest before going out to play croquet or lawn tennis, and then in the evening there'd be card games or musicals — they rather bored me. I must say, though, that there was always something going on."

"But what happened, Laurel?" I asked, weary of her long recital. "Why did you suddenly leave?"

At the time I didn't know how much of the following part of her story to believe, but now I think that most of it was probably true. It seems that the Radcliffes made up what they called a "Woodland Party," which involved riding to a lodge in the woods where lunch would be served.

"I liked the idea," Laurel said. "You know how well I look in my riding habit. We rode all morning — well, anyway, from eleven to one — when we came to the lodge, a gorgeously fitted out log cabin with all the comforts of a good hotel. And what a lunch! The staff had been sent on ahead to prepare it for us. Then after we ate, most of the party went off to take naps. The liquor had been flowing, you see.

"I wasn't sleepy, and neither was Desmond, so we decided to ride up to see the waterfall and one of the caves — those caves are famous. I guess it took longer than we thought, and then it began to rain, just lightly at first, but pretty soon it turned into a terrible downpour. We waited in the cave for a while, but it still didn't let up. Finally we decided it wasn't going to stop, and it was getting late, so we rode back to the lodge, and arrived there soaking wet. The others had all left, even the help, and the rain never stopped. I simply could not face another two hours of riding through the rain, and Desmond said the only thing to do was to stay where we were.

"Well, we were there all night, and when we arrived back at the house in the morning Mrs. Radcliffe made it clear at once that I was persona non grata. I felt awful, but not nearly as bad as I felt when Clara told me that her father had said that I was 'damaged goods' and would never be accepted in society again. This from the man who practically embraced me when he said I was the belle of the ball! He also said that Desmond was to stop seeing me at once. So here I am."

"What did Desmond say?" I asked.

"Nothing. Nothing at all. I never saw him again. He was packed off to his grandparents' place in Maryland. I must say Mrs. Radcliffe was kind enough to let me stay until I recovered from the cold I caught on that wet ride. I guess she didn't want to be held responsible if I died of pneumonia. It wasn't a very pleasant stay, though. I was isolated — sent to Coventry. No one came near me except the doctor and the maids who brought me my meals, and after a week of that I was glad to leave, I can tell you."

"Are you sure you want to stay here, Laurel? We could set up an extra bed in my room at the apartment."

"Oh, no. This will be more comfortable, at least until something better turns up. Leland has money of his own, hasn't he? And he's not bad looking, not bad at all."

"What if he —"

"Finds out about the night at the lodge?" she asked querulously. "I don't see how he can. He doesn't travel in their circles. And besides, it was all very proper, no matter how it looks. Desmond and I slept in separate rooms, and that's the truth. I don't care what the Radcliffes or anyone else thinks. Anyway, Leland is in love with me; you can see that, can't you? Haven't you noticed how he makes a point of sitting close to me in the drawing room? And he never loses an opportunity to take my arm. Last night he said he loved the way my eyes sparkled when he was telling me about the book he's writing. Of course I really wasn't listening to him; I was thinking how good-looking he is, almost as handsome as Desmond. He probably has just as much money, too."

"Yes, I know he's in love with you, Laurel, but —"

"Oh, did I tell you he's taking me to the theater tomorrow night? And we're to go to supper afterward. I'll have to dress up."

"Laurel, listen to me," I said quickly, watching her stifle a yawn. "I think he walks in his sleep, and —"

"What of it?" she asked, starting to rise from the chaise. "Lots of people do. Remember Jeremy?"

"And you should know this," I hurried on. "Miss Prentice told me that the doctors said Leland shouldn't marry —"

"Nonsense!" she interrupted with a dismissive wave of her hand. "She wants him for herself. She loves having a man in the house, even if it is only a nephew. The poor old thing never managed to snag a husband, so she holds on to Leland. I'm sure she made up that business about the doctors. Leland is a perfectly healthy young man. Don't be so gullible, Caro."

With that she slipped gracefully out of the room, leaving me to wonder how much of a blow it would be to Miss Prentice if Laurel did marry Leland.

The next morning when I said good-bye to Miss Prentice I was surprised to feel tears pricking behind my eyes, and as I looked back from the cab that was taking Brad and me the short distance to our new home I felt them again. She was standing at the window where I had first seen her, waving her handkerchief to us.

I think Laurel was still asleep.

I was delighted to see Brad as happy as he was in the days that followed. He liked his work, the apartment was comfortable, and Mrs. Ellis was willing to work for us, but best of all, now Brad had time to devote to Elspeth Dowd.

The rooms in the flat were small, and if their furnishings seemed drab and colorless, they were adequate for our needs. The two dark brown easy chairs on either side of the fireplace in the parlor suited us, the beds were comfortable, and Mrs. Ellis managed not only to cook our meals in the tiny kitchen but also to take care of the laundry and the cleaning. We were fortunate enough to be able to rent the hall bedroom on the floor above us for her, which delighted her. We used to smile at what soon became a nightly ritual with the good woman: She'd come quietly to the parlor door, stand for a moment or two, and if she saw that we were reading or studying she would say apologetically, almost in a whisper: "I'll be on my way up, then," and quietly disappear. We paid her very little, but Brad said he thought she felt safe with us. In any case, she stayed on and on.

"Are you going over to see Elspeth tonight, Brad?" I asked one evening as we were finishing dinner.

"Can't tonight, honey. I've a brief to read, but tomorrow night I'm taking her to see Ada Rehan in that new play. You'll have to meet Elspeth sometime soon, Caro. She's really a wonderful person. She never complained that I was neglecting her this past summer; she understood our difficulties, and was willing to wait."

"Will you be married soon?"

"We are not even officially engaged yet," he said slowly. "It will be at least a year, but sometime . . ."

"You mustn't be concerned about me, Brad. I can always manage. As you know, I have a hundred dollars a month, and I could rent a smaller place, or a room, until I'm earning a decent salary teaching. That should be about two years from now. And who knows, we may get something more when the house is sold and the estate is finally settled."

Brad smiled and shook his head, but all he said was "We'll see."

At the time I was too intent on doing well at the Normal College to be concerned about Laurel, although on the several occasions when Miss Prentice invited Brad and me to dinner I thought she seemed unusually quiet, not at all like the lighthearted girl I had known.

Part IV

Laurel

Chapter 10

I look back on the winter of 1893–94 as one in which I had to be constantly on guard, careful to keep Miss Prentice from suspecting my very serious interest in her nephew. She obviously regarded him as *her* property, no one else's. I modeled my behavior on Caro's: demure, proper, and somewhat retiring, never assertive or flippant. Dear heaven! How boring it was!

I made a point of averting my eyes from Leland whenever his aunt was in the room, and now rarely accepted his invitations to walk in the park or to go to the theater. I thought I made Miss Prentice nervous — or else Leland did, in the way he looked at me, and I also thought that she would have been far happier if I'd moved in with Caro and Brad. She couldn't very well ask me to leave without being rude, though, could she? Anyway, I wonder where I would have gone if she had put me out. I wouldn't dare look up any of the nobs I'd known before;

the Radcliffes had undoubtedly let it be known in society (however subtly) that I was damaged goods, which, to be honest, I was.

Did Miss Prentice suspect that? I had no way of knowing. If Leland did, he most decidedly did not care — and that was important. I certainly didn't love him, but I liked him; I really liked him. He was well-mannered, considerate, and could be delightfully entertaining when he felt like exerting himself. Also, he was rich. On the minus side, he had no interest in the things most of the wealthy people I knew liked to spend their money on: travel, strings of polo ponies, houses in Palm Beach or Bar Harbor, Mediterranean cruises, all those kinds of things. No, he sequestered himself in his study to write books, of all things! I would have understood it if he'd spent his time studying the financial pages.

On a couple of occasions, or maybe three or four, he wouldn't even appear at dinner. He'd send Gordon down with a message that he was at a critical point in his writing and couldn't be disturbed. When I asked Caro if that had happened when she and Brad were there she said no, but then their stay in the Prentice mansion hadn't been very long.

I thought it better not to try to hurry things with Leland, but I couldn't help being somewhat puzzled. I knew, I positively *knew*, that he was in love with me, but when he made no move toward furthering our relationship I began to think he was perfectly happy with the situation as it was. Then I remembered what Caro had said about his not being able to marry. I didn't believe the doctors said that, but still . . .

Anyway, by the middle of January — Christmas had produced no diamond ring from Leland, just a box of lace-edged handkerchiefs — I was so bored that I decided that I would move out, go some place where I'd meet a well-off man who wouldn't hesitate to buy me diamonds.

I probably would have, too, if I had not encountered Vivian Van Schuyler and Walter Wetherell in the park one afternoon. It was a mild day, the January thaw, Miss Prentice had said at lunch, and I was walking slowly, trying to formulate my plans, when I saw the couple approaching me. I nodded and smiled, ready to stop and chat, but they strode right past me, staring straight ahead. The Radcliffes had done their work. A more deliberate cut would be hard to imagine.

That's what they'll all do, I said to myself, and there is nothing, absolutely nothing, that I can do about it.

That night after dinner I excused myself from our usual coffee in the drawing room, pleading a headache, and, still smarting from the afternoon's experience, threw myself on my bed, feeling closer to despair than ever before in my life. I'd been lying there for quite a while, maybe a couple of hours, when I heard a soft knock. My door opened before I could answer and Leland stepped into the room, closing it quietly behind him. He said nothing at first, but sat down on the side of the bed and took both of my hands in his.

"You shouldn't be here, Leland," I said when the silence went on too long. "What would Miss Prentice say?"

"She'll never know," he replied. "She went to bed three-quarters of an hour ago, and is certainly fast asleep by this time."

"Tell me," I said, gently releasing one of my hands from his, "why you came up here. Was it to ask about my headache?"

"You know it wasn't that, Laurel, although I was concerned. No, it was — I have to say it — I want to hold you in my arms. I love you. I've loved you ever since I first saw you. You were coming out of your house. It was months and months ago."

With that he did put his arms around me, pulled me up into a sitting position, and held me close to him. He smelled nice, like an expensive soap, clean and a little bit spicy, not heavy like some perfumes.

"You're so beautiful," he murmured, looking down into my eyes. "I've never seen anyone so lovely in my life. I love you, I love everything about you, your face, your hair, your body . . . Could you — do you think — could you love me?"

"Oh, Leland!" was all I said then, although I felt like asking what took him so long. "I think maybe — but you'll have to give me time," I whispered in true Victorian maiden style.

"Of course, my love, my dearest love," he answered. "All the time you need. I'll come up again tomorrow night." And after a chaste kiss on my forehead, he left as quietly as he had come.

It wasn't much of a love scene, but it was a beginning, the first of a series of nightly visits, during which he would be content to hold me and tell me how lovely I was. I wasn't too surprised; it had taken Leland so long to arrive at that point that I knew it would be some time before the question of marriage arose. I intended to see that it did, however, for at the time I could see no other possible future for me. Desmond, the only man I ever really loved, was lost to me forever, I was outlawed from society, and I had no money except for a miserable hundred dollars a month. Marriage to Leland would be a compromise, I knew that. I didn't love him, but I didn't dislike him — he was charming at times, and as his wife I would be financially secure.

The only strange occurrence during that period was that one night when Leland was leaving me (after the kiss that had become a ritual, but as far as I was concerned was meaningless) I caught a glimpse of Gordon out in the hall before the door closed completely. To give Leland a message? To warn him that Miss P. was awake? I didn't know, and when I asked Leland about it the next time we were alone, he said I must have been mistaken; if Gordon had had a message for him he would have waited at the foot of the stairs, or in Leland's own room.

"You must have seen a shadow, Laurel," he said as he stroked my hair gently. "It couldn't have been Gordon."

What I saw was no shadow, but I let the matter drop.

I saw Caro and Brad occasionally. Miss Prentice invited them to come for dinner about once a fortnight, and I went over to their apartment a few times. It wasn't much of a place, but they didn't seem to care. Brad was too busy trying to get ahead in his firm, and Caro too intent on becoming a schoolteacher as soon as possible. I found myself wishing they wouldn't be so concerned about me. They thought I was frittering my life away, and the last time I was there Brad even suggested that I look for a job.

Somehow or other I survived the long, long spring of 1894 — I'd hate to suffer through another one like it. I was so depressed that I failed to see the change that was taking place in Leland, but I know now that while I was completely wrapped up in myself he was busy making plans, plans that were to have a lasting effect on both our lives.

I had no inkling what was on his mind until one evening late in April when he astonished me by announcing that he wished to spend the night with me.

"I want to sleep with you in my arms, my darling," he whispered, "holding you close to me like this the whole night long."

"But, Leland —"

"Don't worry about Aunt Henrietta, love. I've instructed Gordon to keep a watch on her. I pay him extra — I might say handsomely — for night duty, you see."

"No, Leland," I burst out. "You may not spend the night here. Coming up after dark is bad enough, but don't you see that I'd be compromised, my reputation in ruins, if it ever got out that we'd slept together?"

"How could it, Laurel? Gordon —"

"Oh, any number of ways. The maids aren't stupid, nor are they blind or deaf. I've had some strange looks from Nellie and Mavis already."

"I'll get rid of them," he said angrily.

Neither of us spoke for a moment or two, and then I said slowly, "But, you know, Leland, if we were married you could spend every night with me."

"Oh, my darling, I love you more than life itself, but marriage. . . . Listen, Laurel, listen to me: There's no need for that. Aunt is going to Newport in another month or so, and we'll be free to do what we like for the entire summer."

"No, Leland, absolutely no. It makes no difference whether Miss Prentice is here or not. I will sleep with you only after we are legally married and not before. And if you try to force your way into my bed I'll scream and cry out loud enough to wake the dead."

His face darkened, and when his right arm began to jerk and twitch in a strange way I thought for a moment he was going to strike me. I wondered why he didn't want to get married. Was there some secret in *his* past, or a medical reason, or something else?

When I looked at him again, however, his expression had cleared, the jerking stopped, and he smiled.

"Very well then, my darling," he said softly. "Married we shall be whether Auntie approves or not."

So that was it! He was afraid of Miss Prentice, but I was not.

We both knew that his aunt would not approve, and decided that the only thing to do was to present her with a fait accompli. Leland procured a marriage license, and we planned to go down to the City Hall for the ceremony on the first day of May. Miss Prentice surprised us, though. On the thirtieth of April when we'd finished our after-dinner coffee she took a small notebook from the drawer of the table beside her chair and held it in her hand.

"I wish to talk to both of you about arrangements for the summer," she said in a matter-of-fact way.

I could almost feel myself turn pale, but I managed to smile and nod as if I were expecting a pleasant announcement.

"Yes, Aunt, of course," I heard Leland say. "Will you be going to Newport as usual?"

"I will," she answered evenly, referring to her little notebook. "I shall leave here on the first Monday of June and return early in September, or if the weather is good I may stay until later in the month. That part is all settled. The problem involves you two. I cannot possibly allow you to spend the summer unchaperoned in my house."

She paused and, after drawing a deep breath, asked what we proposed to do.

Before Leland could speak I said that I certainly understood that such a thing would be improper, and that I would move out, making it sound as if I were the soul of propriety.

"And where will you go, Laurel?" she asked.

"Oh, I'll have to decide," I answered. "But there won't be any problem. Caroline and Brad have asked me to live with them, and I have friends in the Berkshires and Bar Harbor who have invited me to visit. You mustn't worry about me, Miss Prentice. You've been more than kind to me all winter and spring. I can never repay you, but it's time I stopped accepting your gracious hospitality."

"Well," she said, looking at me rather doubtfully, "if you're sure you can manage, then my mind will be at rest. Now if you will both excuse me I shall go upstairs. I seem to tire more easily lately than I did in years gone by."

Chapter 11

We slipped out of the house right after breakfast the next morning and drove downtown to the coldest and shabbiest wedding ceremony imaginable. Wait: The word "wedding" is incorrect here, since it invariably conjures up pictures of orange blossoms, flowing lace veils, and long red carpets covering aisles bedecked with flowers. No, what I experienced that May morning was simply a ceremony, every bit as binding as a church affair but devoid of the glamour and fanfare I had for years envisioned for myself.

We took a cab back to the Sixty-ninth Street house without even stopping for a celebratory meal, but at least I had a gold ring on the third finger of my left hand. Leland was quiet as we rode uptown, worrying, I suppose, about how he was to tell his aunt what we had done. It was his problem, and I thought it better not to offer any suggestions. In any case, my mind was occupied with visions of the clothes I could now afford to buy (I was sick and tired of the things I'd been wearing), all charged to the account of Mrs. Leland Prentice.

"I think it would be best if we told her at tea time," Leland said as we drew up in front of the house. "In the meantime I have work to do. Can you amuse yourself, my darling?"

Not exactly the impatient bridegroom, I thought.

I had certainly not expected Miss Prentice to be delighted with the news that we were married, but neither had I anticipated the dreadful reaction it precipitated. Leland waited until tea had been served before telling her, and when he did speak he began reluctantly, I thought, as if he knew he'd be hurting her.

"Laurel won't have to go after all, Aunt," he said nervously. "You see, we were married this morning, so everything will be perfectly proper if she stays here while you are away."

For what seemed an eternity, but couldn't have been more than a minute or two at the most, Miss Prentice stared at him blankly, as if she had trouble understanding what he had said. She looked so pale that I thought she might faint, but she surprised me by setting the teacup she'd been holding carefully on the table in front of her and clasping her hands tightly together in her lap.

"You disappoint me grievously, Leland," she said in a voice that trembled only slightly.

"You see, Aunt, I knew —"

"Yes, Leland, you knew I would be against this marriage, and yet you went ahead with it. You did not consult me, and now I shall not consult you, not about anything at all. Since you seem to be so incompetent in the management of your life I must assume that you will be similarly incompetent in the management of your financial affairs. Tomorrow I will instruct my lawyer to make certain changes in my will; in fact, I shall disinherit you. Of course you will have the interest deriving from your mother's estate, but you will receive nothing, absolutely nothing, from mine."

"Aunt Henrietta, I never wanted —" Leland began.

"Enough! Enough!" she cried, pushing the tea table away from her and getting to her feet. "I shall leave you now so that you can both make plans to leave my house at once. At once, do you hear me? You will not spend another night under my roof. Is that clear?"

Brushing aside the hand Leland held out to help her, she made her way somewhat unsteadily toward the door.

"Aunt, wait, wait a minute!" Leland pleaded. She may have intended to listen to him, because she paused and half turned toward him. A moment later, however, she lay motionless and to all appearance lifeless on the Persian rug.

"A shock to the system, known as a stroke, or apoplexy," Dr. Bellingham said when he finished examining the frail old woman. "No doubt about it. She'll need care around the clock. Do you want me to arrange for day and night nurses, Mr. Prentice?"

"Yes, of course," Leland said quickly. "The best ones available. What brought it on, doctor? She seemed to be in the best of health, and was planning to go to Newport for the summer as usual."

"At her age it could have been anything, or nothing at all. The blood just didn't get to the brain. Mr. Prentice, are you all right? Shall I leave you something to help you sleep? No? Well, be careful not to overexert yourself. There's nothing you can do for her that the nurses can't do."

"How long —" Leland started to ask.

"Hard to say, Mr. Prentice," the doctor cut in. "Sometimes the patient comes out of a stroke without any disability whatsoever, but in other cases the effects can be lasting. She might live for a few days, or for a few years. We'll have to wait and see how she responds to the care she will receive. I'll stop by tomorrow. We may know more by then."

I must admit that I hoped she wouldn't linger. The sooner she died the better, so that Leland and I would be entirely free of her restraining presence. As it was, we seemed to be tied to her and her house more firmly than before. Leland was in and out of her room a dozen times a day until she regained consciousness. When she was able to sit up in a chair he'd keep her company, holding her hand and talking softly to her. Her power of speech was gone, and one side of her face was pulled down, disfiguring her horribly, but her eyes were very much alive, and the malevolent stare she directed at me caused me to avoid the sickroom after I made a few attempts to be kind.

"I seem to upset her, Leland," I said when he asked me to keep her company for an hour or so when he had something he wanted to do. "She either looks at me as if she'd like to kill me or else she closes her eyes and pretends to sleep. She's furious at me, I can see that."

"Well, yes," he muttered, turning away so that I couldn't see his face. "Anyway, the nurse is there." With that he went out, leaving me to make what I would of the entire situation.

The ceremony at City Hall had not changed anything between us. Our marriage remained unconsummated. Maybe, I told myself, it's just as well, since I had no desire to become pregnant. I was puzzled, however, by Leland's behavior. At first I blamed it on his feeling responsible for Miss Prentice's condition, but as the days went by and he withdrew more and more into himself I began to think he was blaming me. He never said that in so many words, but although he was invariably polite and considerate, all the warmth had gone out of his voice when he spoke to me, and his eyes no longer lit up when I entered the room. The nightly visits had ceased completely.

In view of what happened one sultry night early in June, perhaps it was just as well that Leland slept in his own room. I was on my way upstairs — I'd been at Caro and Brad's for dinner — when I heard loud, incoherent, almost guttural sounds coming from the second floor. I flew up the rest of the steps, and as I pushed open the door to Leland's room I saw Gordon struggling to hold my husband down on the bed.

"Go away!" the butler shouted. "Don't come in here!"

"I'm his wife! I will come in!" I cried. "What's wrong with him? Get the doctor!"

Leland's face was contorted and blood oozed from the corner of his mouth as I watched Gordon trying to control the convulsive movements of his entire body.

"Hand me a spoon," Gordon ordered. "Over there on the table. He's bitten his tongue."

I found the spoon, and then stood helplessly by as the terrible convulsions gradually subsided.

"There, it's over," Gordon said after what seemed like an eternity and he was pulling a light blanket up over Leland. "He'll sleep for a couple of hours now. That was a bad attack, believe me."

"An attack of what?" I asked in a whisper, fearful of waking Leland and bringing on a second one. "I have to know, Gordon."

He nodded and, after closing the door quietly, led me to the small sitting room that overlooked the back garden. "He didn't want you to know, ma'am, and if I were you I wouldn't tell him what you saw."

It took a while, but in the end Gordon told me that Leland had a disease once known as the "falling sickness," and more recently as epilepsy, for which no cure was known, and which respectable families tried to keep hidden.

"You see, ma'am," Gordon continued after a pause during which he left me to listen at Leland's door, "it's been kept from him that he has epilepsy. He knows something is wrong, but he thinks he just has some kind of harmless 'spell' once in a while. Part of my job is to look after him, although I really am a butler. I've been with him ever since he was a little boy, and when the doctors told Miss Prentice what was wrong with her nephew she confided in me, knowing somehow she could trust me.

"She's always believed that if it were known that he had epilepsy the family name would be disgraced. Some people keep epileptics locked up, or else put them in institutions. No need for such measures here, though. Mr. Leland is perfectly normal most of the time; you know that yourself. He's clever, too. Be a shame to incarcerate him."

"So that's why Miss Prentice didn't want

him to marry," I said.

Gordon nodded, and then said thoughtfully:

"That's partly her reason, I think. She was afraid he'd pass the disease on to the next generation. But I also think she wanted to keep him to herself since she has no one else. And for the most part he did comply with her wishes. Oh, there were times when he'd stray. He'd see a beautiful girl and think he was in love, but it never came to anything. Then he'd have an attack, and somewhere along the line Miss Prentice persuaded him that marriage was out of the question."

"Until he saw me?"

"Yes, and then you see, ma'am, it became a question of proximity, if that is the right word. He was enchanted, bewitched by you — oh, I think I heard him groan. I'll just go check."

A few minutes later the butler returned to say he'd better stay with Leland, and that I should get some sleep. I nodded and went quietly up to the third floor, but not to sleep. No matter how I tried to banish the image of Leland's agonized, bloody face from my mind, the awful, disgusting picture, like one of an insane monster, kept presenting itself.

No wonder they locked them up. I suppose

I could get the marriage annulled, but where would I go?

At breakfast the next morning Leland seemed to have no memory of the horror of the night before (later Gordon told me that this was often the case) and surprised me by suggesting that I accompany him downtown to Tiffany's to pick out the wedding present he hadn't had time to purchase. I said I'd like that very much and that I'd be ready to leave as soon as I'd spoken to Cook about the meals.

"I'll just look in on Aunt Henrietta while you're doing that, love," Leland said with a smile before running lightly up the stairs.

I saw Cook, and then I found Gordon in his pantry. When I asked him if it would be safe to go downtown with Leland he assured me that it would.

"Perfectly safe, ma'am. He won't have another attack right away. I know the pattern. Yes, go with him. It will do him good."

I think it did me good, too — getting out of the house for one thing, and acquiring a diamond necklace for another. I wasn't completely at ease, though, and kept watching Leland for any change in his facial expression. What would I do if he had an attack in Tiffany's elegant store, or even on the street? I saw no change, however, unless it was in the unusual effort he made to please me. Could he, I wondered, have some sort of vague recollection of having seen me at his bedside? It must be awful, I thought, to have such a terrible disease, even if, as Gordon had said, Leland didn't know he had it.

I thought I ought to make some effort to show Leland how much I appreciated the diamond necklace; it really was quite handsome. Also, he might be offended if I didn't wear it. So I dressed carefully for dinner that night, taking pains with my face and hair and selecting a low-cut black lace evening dress that showed off the necklace to advantage. Black is becoming to me, and the sparkle of the Tiffany diamonds added to the effect I wanted to produce, that of irresistible beauty. I wanted Leland to be glad he'd bought the diamonds for me.

My efforts had the desired effect. "Laurel!" he gasped when I entered the drawing room, "how beautiful! How exquisite you are! You simply radiate beauty, my darling. Come, sit here where I can see you while we have a glass of sherry."

He was acting like the Leland of old, the Leland before his aunt's illness, a welcome change. At least I thought it was welcome, until later that night when he came up to my room for the first time in weeks. I was in bed, just ready to turn off the bedside lamp, when he appeared. He climbed in beside me, whispering endearments and professions of undying love as he took me in his arms, and everything would have been all right, I think, if he'd been content to hold me gently, as he had in the past. That, however, was not his intention.

I know now that I made a mistake in dressing up as I did. I should have been content with something more demure, but that's hindsight. After a few moments Leland's hands were all over me, yanking my nightgown down from my shoulders and exploring my body none too gently. Then he was on top of me, his face inches away from mine. Had the room been dark it might have been different, but in the light of the bedside lamp I saw, or thought I saw, not Leland's regular features, but the distorted ones of the night before, the bloody face of a monster.

I tried to scream, but succeeded only in moaning. I tried to push him away, struggling to get out from underneath him, but his strength far exceeded mine and he didn't relax his hold on me until after he had taken possession of my unwilling body with a penetration that was both fierce and painful.

When it was over he rolled away from me and immediately fell asleep. Sometime later I felt him stir, and fearful of a repeat performance, I pretended to sleep. He slipped out of the bed and after finding his robe, leaned over and kissed me on the forehead. It took all my self-control not to wince, and I did manage to lie still until I heard the door close behind him. That, I thought, was like the kiss of death, but whose death? And what, oh what am I going to do?

The next night when Leland came up to my room I pleaded a headache. His face flushed with anger, and I thought he was going to force himself on me, but after a moment or two he turned and left the room without a word.

I can't go on like this for the rest of my life, I thought. Why did I marry him, for heaven's sake? What have I gained? Money, yes, but is living with a sick old woman and an epileptic husband any kind of life? Is that something to look forward to for years and

years? I felt like a prisoner, and kept murmuring, "I have to get out of here, I have to
think of something" over and over again.

It took me most of the day to decide on a
course of action. At first I thought I'd take
the diamond necklace and whatever money
I could lay my hands on (I knew where
Leland kept a supply of cash for household
expenses) as well as a few clothes and steal
out of the house in the middle of the night.
I would go to one of the better hotels, maybe
the Waldorf, and once established there I
could sell the diamonds one by one whenever
I needed money. And I might meet someone . . .

No, that wouldn't work. Common sense
told me it wouldn't. Suppose I did meet a
wealthy, charming man — he'd just want to
marry me, and I knew enough about big-
amy from Brad's talk to shy away from that
plan.

Brad — I wondered about throwing myself
on his mercy, playing the part of the injured
wife, and asking my brother and sister to take
me in. They probably would have, but I
didn't like the thought of living in their
crowded rooms, and with only a hundred

dollars a month to spend.

In the end I decided to stay where I was, at least for the time being, but on a different basis and according to my own set of rules. Since Miss Prentice was speechless and partially paralyzed, I would announce that I was mistress of the household — I'd already taken over the ordering of the meals — and see that it was run according to my wishes. And most important, because I couldn't bear the thought of any further sexual relations with Leland, I would see a doctor, maybe Bellingham, and persuade him to tell Leland that any more such activity would be bad for my health. Since he knew Leland had epilepsy he might just do as I asked.

I never had the chance to find out. Unfortunately Dr. Bellingham had left for a vacation in Maine, and was not expected back in New York for three weeks. Since I knew no other doctors at that time, I thought the best thing for me to do in order to keep Leland away from me would be to tell him I was pregnant. Later on I could always say that I was mistaken.

I soon found out, however, that there was no mistake; I had merely exchanged one kind of discomfort for another, and for one that would last all of nine months.

Part V

Caroline

Chapter 12

During the early part of Laurel's very difficult pregnancy I spent as much time as I could at the house on Sixty-ninth Street. Not that I enjoyed my visits there — quite the contrary. As I told Brad, it had become the most dismal house imaginable, with Miss Prentice helpless in her room, Leland hardly ever in evidence, and my sister the very picture of despair. She no longer took care with her appearance, some days not bothering to brush her hair or to dress in anything other than a soiled negligee.

The sight of her tear-stained face and unkempt blond hair frightened me, so far removed was it from that of the well-groomed, beautifully dressed sister she had been. Her only interest those days was in food; she was, after all, the mistress of the household, and could order up creamed chicken, potato puffs, all kinds of biscuits, muffins, and breads, pastries and chocolates — anything she fancied. She seemed to crave sweet, creamy foods, and once told me that fruits and vegetables caused her to become nauseated. I could do nothing with her.

Laurel was not the only sorry sight in that house: Poor Miss Prentice seemed to be fading away. I think she tried to smile at times as I sat holding her nerveless fingers in my hand, but since one side of her tired, gray face was drawn down, it was hard to tell. In the past she had enjoyed hearing about my studies, so during the short time I was allowed in the sickroom I would tell her little stories concerning the girls and teachers at the Normal College.

I may have imagined it, but I thought her eyes lit up when I told her that John Rambush, one of the professors, sometimes walked home with me when school was over for the day.

"You'd like him, Miss Prentice," I said, keeping my eyes on her dark ones. "He's teaching history in order to make money while he studies for the bar — you know, the examination that Brad took. And Brad likes him. He thinks he'll do well."

I, too, thought John would do well, but I didn't know whether he singled me out — there were lots of prettier girls in the class — because I was Brad's sister or for myself. Then, one afternoon after classes were over

I was walking down Lexington Avenue thinking I'd rather spend a few hours alone with my books than endure the clouds of despair that hung over the Prentice house, when suddenly I heard footsteps behind me. A moment later John Rambush was beside me.

"Caroline!" he exclaimed breathlessly, "I thought I'd missed you, and I did want to talk to you. Will you have a cup of tea with me? There's a nice little place down on Sixty-fourth Street near Third."

Why, he really does want to see *me*, I thought with some surprise as I accepted his invitation. Wouldn't Laurel have been amazed? He and Brad had known each other in college, and John had stopped in at the flat on several occasions to talk over some point of law that might come up on the bar examination. He never came to see me, or so I thought.

We chatted companionably while we had our tea and toast, laughing over some of the classroom incidents — the girl who thought Lord Byron was an ancient Greek because he wrote about Marathon, the serious young lady who insisted that there was no sense to Homer's line about the "wine dark sea," things like that. Nothing important happened that afternoon, but it was most pleasant, and I was particularly gratified when John smiled across the table at me and said quietly, "I do enjoy being with you, Caroline."

After that he called at the flat more frequently, and several times he and I went out for a stroll, leaving Brad to his briefs. I liked the way he would take my arm when we crossed a street, holding it close to him in a protective way. I couldn't imagine what he saw in me, but I knew I was attracted to him. I liked his kind brown eyes, his ready smile, even his somewhat unruly dark hair, and I missed him on the nights he had to devote to studying for the exam and on the afternoons I spent at the Sixty-ninth Street house.

Laurel was not the only problem there; Leland worried me. He looked dreadful. His beautifully tailored suits hung loosely on him, and his cheeks looked sunken. In fact, his whole face seemed smaller, and even his hair appeared thinner. What a far cry from the handsome young man I had first seen in the garden talking to Caesar!

"It's almost incredible," Brad said when I came home from one of my afternoon visits. "I find it hard to believe that three people could change so radically in such a short time. The stroke would do it to Miss Prentice, yes, but as for Laurel and Leland . . ."

"They are, I think, even more unhappy than Miss Prentice, Brad. Laurel doesn't want the baby, I know that, and Leland is appalled."

"At the sight of Laurel? Or because he knows she doesn't want the child?"

"I don't know. One or the other. It's all so wretched. Something must be done, or else . . ."

"Or else someone will be hurt? Is that what you think, Caro?"

"Yes. It's as if there's a fragile but ominous peace in that house, a silent peace, with no one speaking to anyone else. Laurel talks to me, whines to me, rather, but that's all. I hardly ever see Leland. Should I try to talk to him about Laurel? My school closes for the summer next week, and I'll have more time."

"Anything is worth a try, honey," Brad said with a sigh as he picked up the evening paper.

Gordon told me that before Leland locked himself in his study that Saturday morning he had left orders that he would see no one.

"That's what he does most days, Miss Caroline," the butler whispered as we stood at the foot of the marble staircase. "Sometimes he comes out for a meal, little of which he eats, but not always. And he's drinking! He shouldn't, you know. It's bad for him. I try to keep the brandy away from him, but it's no use. And oh, Miss, it's so sad! He'll grab hold of me every once in a while and say, 'Oh, Gordy, what am I going to do?' It'd break your heart to see the pain in his eyes."

"What, exactly, is his trouble, Gordon?" I asked.

"Ask Miss Laurel — I mean Mrs. Prentice, Miss. She saw one of his attacks. Or wait, the doctor's with her now. Wait for him to come down and let him tell you."

I was puzzled by the abrupt change in the butler's manner, but looking back now, I am inclined to think that perhaps he felt that he would be betraying Leland had he told me what Dr. Bellingham explained so carefully and in such detail.

"We have no cure for epilepsy, Miss Slade," the doctor said after he'd described

150

Leland's attacks. "There is morphine used to quiet the patient if he becomes violent, as some of them do, but that is all. I have trained Gordon to take care of Leland, and for years he's managed quite well. Unfortunately your sister witnessed a severe attack. She's the one I'm worried about, not Leland. He'll live out his life, but his wife — he shouldn't have married, you know."

"Yes, Miss Prentice said that last summer when I was in Newport."

"You should take your sister away, Miss Slade," he said. "Get her out of this house, at least until the child is born. Otherwise she'll either lose her mind or else do away with herself.

"You see, when she saw Leland in the throes of an attack she was taken completely by surprise. Here was her husband, a handsome, personable, gentle man, thrashing around on the bed, uttering guttural sounds, bleeding from the mouth, his face a grotesque mask, and then suddenly subsiding into a deep sleep — a Jekyll and Hyde situation.

"He may not remember anything about the attack; they often don't. Or he might have a vague recollection of feeling slightly ill. I don't know. Your sister, however, has been unable to erase the image of Leland's deformed, bleeding face from her mind, and when he demanded his conjugal rights, literally raping her, she was not only sickened but also terrified. Naturally I've told Leland to stay away from her, and he has, but every time she hears a step on the stairs she panics, thinking it's he, coming to force himself on her again. Your sister will not be able to stand the strain, Miss Slade. Get her out of here if you want her to live."

"I'll try, but where —"

"You mentioned Newport. What about Miss Prentice's cottage? I understand she had planned to spend the summer there, so it should be fully staffed and ready for occupancy. The sea air would be good for Mrs. Prentice. Speak to Leland about it. He has Miss Prentice's power of attorney, and can make any necessary arrangements."

Between us, Dr. Bellingham and I persuaded Leland to let me take Laurel to Newport for the summer. It wasn't easy. "She's my wife," he said more than once, "and she should be here with me." Then he'd shake his head and say: "But maybe I'm not good for her just now." I felt sorry for him then, but I knew what needed to be done.

I honestly did not want to spend the summer taking care of Laurel. It would mean not seeing John for weeks and weeks, but school was over, and I could think of no good reason why I shouldn't go to Newport.

Almost from the moment we stepped aboard the *Priscilla* Laurel began to improve, and when she saw the grand stairway with its rich carpet and elaborate decorations a faint smile appeared on her lips for the first time in weeks. She was not too pleased when she saw the chamber pot under the berth, but *I* was pleased as I watched her prepare for dinner that night. She had washed and arranged her hair before we left Sixty-ninth Street, and by the time she finished applying her creams, lotions, and powders she was almost like the old Laurel. Her pregnancy was not far enough advanced to be noticeable, and when I finished fastening the innumerable hooks and tiny buttons on her peach-colored dress she looked almost ready to step out on the dance floor. Two days ago I would never have believed such a change possible.

As I stood beside her in front of the mirror in my simple blue silk I looked so plain that

I thought I could hear Mamma sigh and say, "Oh, Caroline, what on earth am I going to do with you?"

Heads turned as we entered the *Priscilla*'s large, ornate dining salon and were shown to one of the smaller tables against a paneled wall. That had certainly not happened to me on my trip the previous summer.

"It is really quite elegant," Laurel said with a satisfied smile when we were seated. "I had no idea the Fall River Line ran to such luxury. Of course the silverware isn't sterling, but it's good quality, and these little table lamps with their floral motifs — they're a nice touch."

As I watched her enjoying the evening I marveled at the change in her, and suddenly wondered why neither Brad nor I nor Dr. Bellingham had thought of removing her from the Prentice house sooner. Then another thought occurred to me: Here I was taking her to another Prentice house. What awaits us there, I wondered.

We had finished our shrimp remoulade and were starting on the lobster Newburg when the waiter appeared at our table with a bottle of champagne in a frosted bucket of ice and handed Laurel a card. At her questioning look he nodded to a dark-complected gentleman who was dining alone at a table across the salon from us.

"He sends this with his compliments, madam," the waiter said, "and hopes you will enjoy it."

"Who is he, Laurel?" I asked.

"I've no idea," she answered quickly, tearing the card in half and dropping it on the floor. "Please return the champagne to the gentleman," she said to the astonished waiter. "We do not drink alcoholic beverages," she lied.

The sender, whoever he was, realized what was taking place and was on his way out of the dining salon well before the waiter reached his table.

"You did recognize that man, didn't you Laurel?" I asked when we were back in our stateroom. "Who is he?"

"How could you tell, Caro?" she asked irritably as she sank down into the small armchair next to her berth. "Oh, it doesn't matter. Actually he was a friend of Desmond's, Roddy Cameron, and he thinks he's irresistible to women. He was in the riding party I told you about, and no doubt thinks that since I've been blackballed by society

I'll be happy to accept his advances. Some nerve!"

"He had a peculiar face," I said. "So long and narrow, and such a pointed chin."

"Aristocratic, *he* thinks," Laurel said with a yawn as she kicked off her shoes. "I know it's early, but I'm tired. Are these beds comfortable?"

She fell asleep quickly that night, but I lay awake for some time, wondering about the strange-looking Mr. Cameron and hoping we'd seen the last of him. Then my thoughts turned to John Rambush. At first he had seemed only mildly disappointed that I was going to be away from the city for most of the summer, but the night before I left I realized that his feelings were considerably stronger than that. He delighted me by inviting me to have dinner with him at Delmonico's grand restaurant down on Beaver Street, where Papa and Mamma used to dine with clients of the bank.

"Get out your gladdest rags, Caro," Brad said when he heard where we were going. "You'll be in with all the swells at that place."

Fortunately Mamma had seen to it that I had a few summer evening dresses (bought in preparation for festivities in the cottage in the Berkshires), which I had never worn. I chose the simplest one, an organza in a delicate apricot color, low cut at the neckline, neatly fitted at the waist, and with a skirt so full it swished when I walked.

Quite a change from a shirtwaist and school skirt, I thought as I studied my reflection in the mirror. The hairdresser around the corner from us had pinned my hair up in such a way that I looked taller than my five feet four inches, and she also persuaded me to apply a minimal amount of powder and rouge to what I had always considered my nondescript face. You look better than I would have thought possible, Caroline, I said to myself, turning away from the mirror.

I really must have looked nice, for when I appeared in the parlor, carrying my matching silk coat, even my brother was impressed.

"My!" he exclaimed. "Cinderella goes to the ball! No fooling, Caro, you look stunning!"

"A tall, slim princess," John murmured as he held the coat for me. "Don't wait up for us, Brad. The pumpkins don't appear until after midnight."

This is how Laurel must feel all the time, I thought as I basked in his admiring glances during the ride downtown in the cab John had had waiting at the door. Sometime during the trip he took my hand in his, making

157

me wish I could take off my long white kid gloves so that I could feel his warmth and tenderness.

"Yours is such a delicate beauty," he murmured as we drew up in front of the Renaissance-style building with the famous Pompeian columns gracing its entrance.

The rest of the evening was like a dream that passed all too rapidly; we dined in splendor in the soft light of a pink-shaded table lamp on shrimp, squab, mushrooms, and tiny peas, accompanied by one of the most delicious French wines I ever tasted, and finished off with the baked Alaska for which the restaurant was famous. Of course we talked: I filled him in on what he didn't already know about our family, and I learned how both his parents had succumbed to typhoid fever a few years earlier, leaving him a small inheritance.

"It's not much, Caroline, barely enough to live on, so it's up to me to make a success of the law. An assistant professor of history at the Normal College doesn't rate much in the way of salary, but it's a job that gives me time to study, as you know."

He looked as if he were about to say something further, but just then the waiter came with our coffee, so it wasn't until he was saying good-night to me in our parlor that he returned to the subject.

I was beginning to thank him for the splendid evening when he suddenly took me in his arms, holding me so that he could look down at my face.

"I can't ask you to marry me yet, my dearest," he said softly, "but I can ask you to wait — it won't be too long — until I am in a position to support you in style. I love you, Caroline, I love you! Do you —"

He broke off when I smiled and nodded, and the next moment his lips were pressed on mine with a fervor beyond anything I had ever imagined. It was well after midnight when he left me, and as I lay in the narrow berth on board the *Priscilla* it seemed to me that I could still feel his arms holding me, holding me so tenderly, so firmly . . .

Chapter 13

Surprisingly, Laurel adjusted readily, almost complacently, to the quiet life at Corinth. I had been afraid she'd find fault with the old-fashioned gloominess of the place, and complain about the lack of entertainment. On the contrary, she was genuinely interested in the house itself, in its furnishings, and the hundreds of objets d'art that one saw on every table, shelf, and mantelpiece.

"I suppose the old lady will leave all this to Leland, won't she?" she asked after we'd been in Newport for a few days and she'd had time to go through all the rooms. "If she does — and who else is there? — I would be able to get away from him for summers, at least. He always stays in town, doesn't he?"

When I nodded she continued, almost as if she were thinking aloud. "I could come here in May and stay until October. That would give me four — no, five — months away from him. Now if I can only think of some way to get through the rest of the year

. . . maybe I could persuade Dr. Bellingham to say my health was weakened by childbirth and can't stand the cold weather, so he advises me to spend the winter months in the South. That might just be possible, and Leland could easily afford it. Oh, if only I weren't going to be saddled with an infant!"

At that time I knew very little, practically nothing, about pregnancy or childbirth. Mamma had been reticent on the subject; when I started to menstruate she merely said that it was something that women did. Somewhere along the line, probably mostly from my reading, I began to understand what was involved in sexual intercourse, even to realize that it could be the most satisfying and beautiful experience a woman could have.

Would Laurel have enjoyed it, I wondered, if she hadn't seen Leland in the midst of an epileptic attack? She might have, but she still would have resented being pregnant. People like Laurel shouldn't marry, I thought. They'd go through life thriving on adulation, promising pleasure and ending up causing pain. How cruel that sounds! But it's what Laurel has done; look how miserable she's made Leland's life. And he was so deeply in love with her. . . .

"Maybe I'll put the child up for adoption,"

she said now, so softly that I almost didn't hear her.

"Laurel! You wouldn't!"

"Oh yes I would! Or you can have it. After all, you'll be its aunt. Come on, let's go out in the garden. I had Anton bring down some old wicker chairs I found in the attic. We need new ones, and new cushions, too, but these will do for now."

She did order new garden chairs, along with a matching table, so that on fine days we could have tea in that peaceful spot, which is what we were doing when Roddy Cameron called.

Laurel was leaning back on her cushions with her eyes closed, her face protected from the warm July sun by the floppy brim of an old straw hat she'd found in one of the attics. I suppose it had belonged to Miss Prentice, or maybe to her mother. It was not particularly pretty; the silk flowers that decorated the crown were faded, and the straw itself a bit crushed. On anyone else it would have been ridiculous, but on Laurel it looked like a milliner's triumph.

From time to time I glanced up from my book — I'd found a copy of *The Mill on the*

Floss on one of Miss Prentice's shelves —
and thought how much my sister had im-
proved in the short time we'd been at
Corinth, a thought invariably followed by
worry over what would happen to her when
we returned to New York in September.
Leland missed her, I knew; at least I thought
he must since he wrote to her four or five
times a week, letters she tore up and threw
away almost as soon as they arrived.

I was careful to slip John's letters into my
pocket before she came down to breakfast —
I wanted no questions from her — and I
would write to him in the privacy of my room
after she had gone to bed. I was wondering
whether I'd hear from him the next afternoon when the screen door banged, and Jessie, the parlormaid, came toward us,
followed by a tall man.

"Mr. Cameron, to see Miss Slade," she
said, stepping to one side to allow him to
pass. "Will you be wanting more tea, Miss?"
she asked, and turned to go back to the house
when I nodded.

From the puzzled expression on Roddy
Cameron's long, lean face I knew he hadn't
heard of Laurel's marriage. There'd been no
notice of it in the papers. He was also probably wondering how the lovely Laurel Slade
could have such a mouse for a sister.

"Dear me!" he exclaimed in a high-pitched voice as Laurel sat up straight and glared at him. "Dear me! I seem to have blundered —"

"Indeed you have, Roddy Cameron," Laurel said sharply. "Didn't I make it clear on the boat that I have no interest whatever in you?"

"Nor I in you, my dear," he replied. "I am merely the bearer of a message from poor, lovesick Desmond. My word, you are beautiful, Laurel, even when flushed with anger!"

"Just go, Roddy! Go!"

"Yes, of course, my dear girl. But first the message must be delivered: At the homecoming party for the Radcliffes — they'd been to Europe, you know, of course you know — Desmond took me aside. He was most despondent, and had trouble getting the words out, but this is what he said: 'If you ever see Laurel tell her I still adore her.' There, message delivered!"

"Go away, Roddy, go away!" Laurel was almost shouting.

"Yes, yes, I am going. What a shame, though, to leave this lovely scene. Really, it should be painted and called *An Afternoon in the Garden*. One of those Frenchies could do it."

Then, with a slight, mocking bow, he left,

twirling his cane as he walked with more than a hint of a swagger toward the house. He reminded me of an actor playing the part of a dandy in that play with Mrs. Malaprop in it. What was it? *The Rivals* or *The School for Scandal?*

A few minutes later, as if there had been no interruption to our afternoon, Jessie brought out a fresh pot of tea, Laurel smiled at me, and the sun continued to shine on the flowers that nodded their heads over the broken column.

Chapter 14

"Caro, where is the little bronze horse that stood on the table in the hall?" Laurel asked the next morning as she came in to the breakfast table. "Have you seen it? It's such a darling little thing. I was wondering if that, too, came from Greece. But where is it?"

Jessie hadn't seen it, and Anna, who did the cleaning, remembered that on the previous day she had simply lifted it up, dusted it, and put it back on the table. Laurel frowned, and then called Jessie back into the breakfast room.

"Jessie," she said quietly, "when Mr. Cameron left yesterday afternoon did he go through the house and out the front door?"

"Yes, ma'am," the girl replied. "I think so. Cook was restin' so I was makin' the tea when he came through the garden door. He waved to me from the passageway and said he'd see himself out."

"That's where the little horse went," Laurel said as soon as we were alone. "Roddy simply picked it up and slipped it into his pocket. I suppose he'll sell it; he was always short of money. I know he borrowed from Desmond. That's too bad, though. I really liked that little horse."

I was reminded of the old treasure chest she'd had when we were growing up. The bronze horse would have been larger than the rest of the items in her collection, but still . . .

As the summer progressed, morning walks on the beach, long, lazy afternoons in the sun-soaked garden where Laurel dozed and I made my way through volume after volume of George Eliot's works, and evenings spent in front of the fire Jessie would light to ward off the chill became the pattern of our days. Boring as it may sound, we both thrived on that self-imposed regimen. Once Laurel had made her "escape from Leland plans," as she called them, she seemed more content than I had known her to be in a long time.

The uneventful days slipped by with little variation in our schedule until one morning in mid-August when I returned from a solitary walk (Laurel said it was too windy and cool for her) to find my sister talking to a stranger in the drawing room.

"Oh, Caro," she said as soon as she saw me, "I'd like you to meet Desmond Radcliffe. Desmond, this is my sister, Caroline."

The tall, athletic-looking man who stood up to acknowledge the introduction was not only handsome but also had one of the warmest, most engaging smiles I had ever seen. He had the regular features one saw in pictures of a matinee idol, but he looked more interesting than they ever did because of the alert look in his eyes. What a stunning couple he and Laurel must have made, I thought as I sat down in the chair he drew up for me.

"As I suspected, Caro," Laurel said with a trace of amusement in her voice, "Roddy lost no time in telling Desmond where he found me. But what good will it do now, Desmond? I've told you I'm not only married, but also more than two months pregnant."

"Yes, I understand the situation, Laurel," he said calmly, "but I see no reason why I shouldn't visit you from time to time."

"No, Desmond —"

"Don't, please, forbid me to come."

"What will your family say?"

"Nothing, because they won't know about it. I'm staying with a great-aunt who has a so-called cottage about a mile from here."

"Very convenient," Laurel drawled, "but I still don't think . . ."

At that point I excused myself, thinking I'd better allow them to argue it out by themselves. Would Laurel give in, I wondered as I went upstairs, and permit him to call? I was afraid she would; she seemed to be enjoying his company, almost reveling in his adoration, and I could think of no way of preventing his coming.

What will happen, I asked myself, if Leland arrives unexpectedly as he did the previous summer, and finds Desmond here? It's not likely, but it is possible.

Desmond won, and during those incredibly lovely summer days he became a steady visitor to Corinth, generally coming in time for tea, which we had in the garden as often as possible. It was there that Leland found us laughing over a story Desmond was telling about his great-aunt's fear of her cook.

"Great-aunt Letitia is quite a despot herself," he was saying, "and to see her actually trembling — oh, hello, we have company."

It is difficult for me to remember the exact sequence of the events that took place in the next few minutes. It all happened too quickly for the details to be clear in my mind, but this is what I recall.

From the moment I saw the expression on Leland's face I was frightened. It was not so much the look of an angry man as it was of a person out of control. His mouth hung open a bit, his cheeks were flushed, and when he tried to speak only strange, unpleasant sounds were audible, sounds somewhere between groans and grunts. When Desmond stood up, shielding Laurel with his body as he did so, Leland struck out at him, knocking him off balance for a moment. Desmond righted himself just in time to dodge another wild blow from the enraged Leland and, moving quickly, aimed a hard fist at his attacker's head just behind his ear. Leland stood still, eyes closed, and then slowly, ever so slowly, sank to his knees and toppled over, hitting his head on the leaning section of the marble column.

I don't know what we would have done if Gordon hadn't come running down the path. He had evidently accompanied Leland on the trip and, like the well-trained servant he was, had waited in the house while his master joined us in the garden. He took charge at once, ordering me to take Laurel inside and saying he would need Desmond's help in getting Leland to bed.

"A terrible attack," I heard him mutter. "If you would be so good as to take his feet, sir, I can manage his shoulders."

I hurried a pale and frightened Laurel into the drawing room and closed the door so that we wouldn't see Leland being carried upstairs. I don't know how long I sat there, watching Laurel walking aimlessly around the room, picking up and putting down pieces of Miss Prentice's bric-a-brac, but after a while the door opened and Desmond appeared looking shaken.

"Laurel darling," he said, as he folded her into his arms, "are you all right?"

"Is he dead?" she asked in a muffled voice.

"No," Desmond replied. "He's all right. That fellow, Gordon — who is he, anyhow, his valet? — says he'll take care of him, and that he'll almost certainly sleep through the night. Can you imagine? He said that he probably won't remember anything about the fight in the morning."

Between us, Laurel and I explained Gordon's position and the seriousness of Leland's epilepsy (which apparently my sister had not done) to Desmond.

"You mean no one told you about

Leland's disease before you married him?" he exclaimed.

Laurel burst into tears. "No, no one did," she sobbed. "And you know, Desmond, it's really your fault that I married him."

"Darling! What on earth —"

"If you hadn't taken me on that horseback trip, none of this would have happened. I wouldn't have been ostracized, left out, snubbed, desperate for someone who could support me — and now look at me!"

Desmond stood completely still, speechless, watching her as she dabbed at her eyes with one of her lace-edged handkerchiefs and straightened her shoulders. She seemed to have reached a decision.

"You'd better go, Desmond. Yes, please go. Nothing you can do will help me now," she said calmly.

"I will always love you," he said softly. He stared at her steadily for a long moment before turning and walking slowly toward the door. He did not look back.

I was in the kitchen going over the day's menus with Cook the next morning when Leland came downstairs. The lump on his head, partly covered by his neatly combed hair, and a swollen lower lip were the only signs of yesterday's fracas that I could see.

"Oh, there you are, Caroline," he said hurriedly. "I must talk to you. Laurel's still asleep, and I can't make any sense out of what Gordon tells me."

"I was just about to go for an early walk on the beach," I said after a quick glance at the apprehensive look on Cook's face. "Would you like to come with me?"

"Yes, of course. But, Caroline, I have to know what happened."

I made no reply until we were down near the water's edge, when I asked him what Gordon had said.

"Oh, some nonsense about me tripping and bumping my head, but I don't remember that. I thought I saw a man, a stranger, holding Laurel's hand, and then, oh, I don't know . . ."

"You came out into the garden, Leland, where Laurel and I were having tea. The flagstones on the path there are uneven, and you stumbled on one of them. You did fall, and that's what gave you that ugly bump on your head."

"But the man, Laurel — I mean Caroline — who was he? Was he real? Did I imagine him?"

"That bump," I said carefully, "that bump

is really a nasty one, and could have caused you to have weird dreams. I know that after I'd fallen down the stairs when I was a child I dreamed that the witch in "Hansel and Gretel" had pushed me, and when I got to the bottom of the stairs another witch was there, laughing and telling me to go back up to the top so that the first witch could push me down again. I had a huge bump on my head then, too."

"I'm not a child, Caroline. I know — I know that I have memory lapses. They make me feel strange, and then I fall asleep, and when I wake up it's all a blur. And I can't understand why Aunt Henrietta was so against my marrying; any normal man wants to marry. Look at history's heroes: King Arthur, Napoleon, Washington — they all wanted wives. Why shouldn't I?"

Were they right, I wondered, Miss Prentice, Gordon, and Dr. Bellingham, in keeping the truth from Leland? That they acted out of kindness was certainly the case, but did they choose the wisest course? At the time, however, all I could think of to say to Leland was that I thought Miss Prentice wanted to keep him to herself.

"She hasn't anyone else, you see, Leland, and sometimes old ladies, especially spinsters, can be extremely selfish, and put their own happiness ahead of that of others," I concluded.

A short, bitter laugh was his only reply.

To Laurel's dismay, Leland and Gordon stayed with us for the rest of the summer, and the old house, especially on rainy days, was as gloomy as the city house had been. Sunny days were better; the beach, with its ever-changing tides and colors, and the lovely garden with its steady progression of blooms and scents gave me, at least, some respite from the unhappiness within the walls of Corinth.

My sister had taken to spending the better part of each day in bed, coming downstairs only for dinner and retiring soon after it was over. I wanted desperately to go back to New York and leave the others to themselves, but although I was bored and almost as unhappy as Laurel and Leland were at times, I could not bring myself to abandon them.

Nothing of much importance happened during that time, but there was one incident worth noting: On two or three occasions I ordered a carriage and had myself driven in to the shops to buy incidentals, stationery, ribbons, face cream, and other small necessities. Twice Leland accompanied me, spending his time in the town's only bookstore while I made my purchases. On our last trip, shortly before we returned to New York, we were about to start back for Corinth when my eye was caught by a particularly beautiful glass vase in a shop window. I paused to admire it, and had called Leland's attention to its vibrant colors when I noticed what looked like our missing bronze horse standing near it. I gasped, and Leland, thinking I'd fallen in love with the vase, offered to buy it for me.

"Oh, no," I said, "not the vase. It's the little horse next to it that delights me."

"Then you shall have it, Caroline," he said, and before I could stop him he hurried into the shop. He gave no indication of recognizing it; I supposed he hadn't spent enough time at Corinth to be familiar with all of his aunt's possessions. I've no idea what he paid for it, and I never told him its story; I simply gave it to Laurel, who laughed.

"Didn't I tell you Roddy would sell it?" she said. "Wait till I tell Desmond! By the way, word came while you were gone that the old lady died last night. I suppose that means we'll all have to go back to the city for the funeral."

So, I thought, she must be in touch with Desmond, one way or another.

Chapter 15

Once she was back in the city house Laurel was so nervous — distraught might be a better word — that I decided to stay with her for a few days. She surprised me in that she refused to sleep in her own bed, but chose to move over to the smaller chamber, the one that had been Brad's, on the other side of the sitting room.

"I know *you* won't mind being in my old room, Caro," she said, removing a fresh nightgown carefully from one of the drawers, "but it has bad memories for me, and I'm afraid I'd just lie awake all night. We'll leave both doors to the sitting room open so that you'll hear me if I call. And you'll stay, won't you? You don't mind, do you?"

I did mind. I minded terribly. I wanted to sleep in my own bed in the apartment on Lexington Avenue. I wanted to see Brad, and oh, how I wanted to see John! On the other hand I felt wretched that I hadn't been more of a comfort to Miss Prentice when she was ill. If I'd only been there to hold her hand when she was close to death, I'd have felt better. We'd established a bond between us, respect on both sides, and the difference in age did not seem to matter. I know she liked me, she may even have loved me in her own way. I was indebted to her, and the only way I could think of repaying her now was to keep Laurel under control until after the good woman was properly laid to rest.

"I'll stay until after the funeral, Laurel," I promised, "but then I must —"

"Oh, one more night after that, Caro," she begged. "I'll be all right by that time."

At the time I didn't know what she meant by "all right." I merely assumed that by then she'd have dealt with her fears and anxieties. That is exactly what she did mean, but her method of doing so was far from anything I could have imagined.

Immediately after Miss Prentice's frail body was interred in the family mausoleum in Woodlawn Cemetery we went back to the house for the funeral meats and the reading of the will. Aside from a few bequests to servants and charitable organizations everything went to Leland — everything, that is, except the house in Newport, which she left to me, along with a trust fund for its upkeep. I was thunderstruck, but no one else appeared to be the least bit surprised.

Laurel received nothing, but she didn't seem to care. When she smiled sweetly at me I thought she was rejoicing at my good fortune, and I took her hand in an effort to assure her that her plans for spending summers at Corinth would not be disrupted. Ah, me . . .

"I'm exhausted," she said as the lawyer began to pack up his papers before leaving. "If you'll excuse me, Leland, I'll lie down for a while before dinner."

"Of course, my love," he said gently. "It's been a long, long day, and you need your rest."

It's so sad, I thought, seeing the longing look in his eyes as he watched her go slowly up the wide staircase. Will she ever be able to make him happy? I wondered. Knowing Laurel as I did, I should have realized that she wouldn't even try.

Perhaps it was the emotional strain that so often accompanies death and its attendant ceremonies, or it might have been worry about Laurel's future that caused me to lie awake for some time that night before I fell into a sound sleep. Some time later I awoke with a start to see light streaming in through the sitting room door, and a moment later Leland burst into my room, shouting that Laurel was gone and that I had better tell him where she went.

"You know!" he said angrily. "You helped her get away! I saw you holding her hand! I know you helped her!"

"Leland! Laurel's in the other room. We changed beds."

"She's gone, I tell you! Don't lie to me! Where did she go?"

"Let me look!" I cried, struggling to get up. "I told you we changed beds —"

"She's not there, I tell you," he said, pushing me back onto the bed. "Tell me where she went! I'll make you tell me!"

When he finally let me get up and look in the other room for myself, I was aghast.

"See," he gloated, "the bed's empty, and there's her blue nightgown. I looked in the other room first, but you were asleep."

"Maybe Gordon saw her," I said in desperation.

"I gave Gordy the night off. Now listen, Caroline, I know Laurel confided in you; she never did in me. So tell me what she said she was going to do, where she was going."

"I don't know, Leland. She never said a word."

That was true: She hadn't said anything to me about leaving, but I was sure that she'd arranged to go off with Desmond. I'd suspected earlier that she'd been in touch with him — oh, I should have *known!*

Leland kept at me for what seemed like hours, accusing me over and over again of helping her get away, and finally he threatened to use force to make me tell where she'd gone. I couldn't believe my ears. He wasn't having an epileptic fit, not then, anyway, but he was so angry that he might just as well have been.

"Get dressed," he ordered after a while. "We'll look for her."

He waited at the door with his back to me while I put on the clothes I had taken off a few hours earlier — I didn't dare take the time to search for clean ones — and in a few minutes he was propelling me down the stairs.

When we reached the first floor he paused for a moment, but he didn't let go of me.

"One last chance, Caroline. Where did my wife go?"

"Leland, I have no idea. I don't —"

"Very well. You'll have plenty of time to think it over all alone, and in the dark."

With that he opened a heavy wooden door I had never noticed before and, taking a firmer grip on my arm, guided me down a flight of stone steps to what I realized must be the cellar. When we reached the bottom he laughed, a crazy laugh, more like a cackle than anything else.

"Scary, isn't it?" he asked. "When I was a boy I used to come down here to frighten myself, and now I'm going to leave you to frighten yourself into telling me the truth."

He squeezed my arm painfully before letting go of me and running lightly up the stairs — he was evidently quite familiar with them — laughing and uttering strange, undistinguishable sounds.

Was this the man I had felt such compassion for earlier in the evening? The kind, gentle companion who had gone on shopping trips with me in Newport? This monster, this cruel . . .

"Oh, my God!" I whispered as I heard the heavy door slam, "if he has an attack, and maybe he's been having one all along, then he won't remember where he put me. . . ."

I shivered and stood perfectly still, not wanting to reach out for fear of touching something alive. When my legs would no longer hold me up, I sank down on the cold stone floor and cried.

After what seemed like hours and hours I saw a faint streak of light, a long, narrow streak, directly in front of where I was crouching, but some distance away, and with hands outstretched as I took small, careful steps I more or less felt my way toward it. Someone, possibly Leland, had nailed a piece of heavy black material over one of the cellar windows, and for a moment I thought I could smash the glass and make my escape either into the street or through the garden. I'd lost all sense of direction by that time, but in the end it didn't really matter which way the window faced because when I ripped the cloth away I was confronted with a series of steel bars placed too close together to permit either entrance or egress. As the light grew stronger I was able to see that just outside the window a stone-lined passage ran, like the moats around medieval castles, but of no help to me whatsoever.

Thinking there might be a cellar door somewhere that led to the outside, I began to move around the periphery of the large room. One section seemed to be used for storage, and contained numerous pieces of discarded furniture as well as tightly sealed cartons and barrels. On a shelf not far from the window I found an assortment of carpenter's tools, all in a jumble, among them a box of candles, the thick, stubby kind that a plumber would use, and right beside them a box of wooden matches. I almost couldn't believe my luck.

When I had lit one of the candles, I still could not see everything in that cavernous cellar, but the sight of the enormous furnace reminded me of how, in our old house down in Harrison Street, the furnace man used to come in a special door from the outside that opened directly into the cellar. There must be one here, I thought; they'd never want him tramping through the kitchen and using the stairs down which Leland had dragged me.

There must be a door, there must be a door, I kept saying to myself as I felt my way along one of the walls, hoping against hope that my fingers would come in contact with a doorknob, that it would turn easily, that the door would open, and that I'd be able to step outside. Of course it didn't happen that way; the door I eventually found had never been used by any furnace man, nor, I am sure, by many other people. It was in the wall I thought was in the rear of the building, a heavy metal door, fastened with a large sliding bolt that took all my strength to pull back.

The door creaked as it swung open, and at first I thought it might lead to another room, a wine cellar, perhaps. But then, with the aid of the flickering light of my candle I was able to see what appeared to be a tunnel, a dark, brick-lined tunnel, four or five feet wide and somewhat higher. Why have a tunnel, I wondered, and where did it lead? It must — and then suddenly I remembered Miss Prentice's puzzling remark about a "connection" between the two houses, and how her mother had teased her father, saying he never should have read *The Mysteries of Udolpho*. That was it! The tunnel would lead me to our former mansion. . . .

It *has* to lead to the Sixty-eighth Street house, I thought, and started on my way into the darkness ahead of me. It would come out in our cellar, I reasoned, and I knew where the stairs were; I'd had to go down there after Caesar several times when the big cat went exploring and wouldn't come up when I called.

The floor of the tunnel was damp, and I was taking my time, being careful not to slip, when I heard a noise behind me. I knew immediately it was Leland. I had left the metal door open, and he would have seen it as soon as he reached the bottom of the stairs — how stupid of me!

"Caroline! Caroline!" resounded through the narrow corridor, the echoes seeming to bounce off the walls.

"Caroline, you bitch, you traitor, I'm coming to get you!"

Terror such as I had never known before gripped me and I broke into a run, causing my candle to go out. I dropped it and, extending my arm, felt my way along the wall on my right. It had just occurred to me that the door at the far end of the tunnel might be locked — I'd never even noticed it when I was looking for Caesar — when I ran blindly into it, hitting it with such force that it swung open. Sobbing for breath I burst through, slammed it shut behind me, and turned the big key in the lock. God knows why it had been left unlocked, I thought.

Subsequent events are not exactly clear in my mind; I vaguely remember hurrying up the stairs to the first floor, climbing out one of the kitchen windows, running down the side alley used by the delivery boys, and out onto Sixty-eighth Street. I must have paused someplace to catch my breath, but I have no recollection of that. I do know that as I hurried over to Lexington Avenue and down to

Sixty-fifth Street I thought I could still hear Leland's voice calling over and over again: "Caroline, Caroline . . ."

Now that I think of it, I must have looked like a sight as I ran: My hair was wild, my dress filthy from the dust of the cellar and the tunnel, and my face was probably dirty. Fortunately it was still very early in the morning, and there were few people about to turn and stare at me. If a policeman had seen me I'm sure he would have taken me for a thief and arrested me. As it was, when Brad opened the door in response to my insistent ringing and banging he hardly recognized me before I collapsed at his feet.

Part VI

Laurel

Chapter 16

We had left Corinth in such a mad rush to get to the old lady's funeral that, fortunately for me, no orders for the closing up of the house had been given. The servants accepted my return without question; after all, I was Mrs. Prentice, and for all they knew the wife of the new owner. Nor did they seem surprised at the extent of my exhaustion, which caused me to stay in bed for three days after my arrival.

I really was at the end of my strength. Planning my escape from Leland with Desmond had been fun, but putting the plan into action was something else entirely. We had worked it all out before Miss Prentice's death, but we hadn't expected to execute it so soon. Desmond is really quite resourceful, though, and when everything was speeded up he rose to the occasion. He had a cab waiting for me around the corner of Sixty-ninth Street on Fifth Avenue when I slipped out of the house shortly after mid-

191

night, and we spent the rest of the night and most of the next day in seclusion in a small hotel on the West Side. In the evening we boarded the *Priscilla*, the same boat Caro and I had taken to Newport earlier in the season. This time, however, we had our meals served in our stateroom, not wanting to run the risk of being recognized.

When I asked Desmond what we would do for money — I had only about fifty dollars, what Leland called my "pin money" — he laughed and told me not to worry. He had the income from a trust fund set up by his grandparents, he said, and expectations from his great-aunt Letitia, whose favorite he was.

"We can live in style, my darling Laurel," he said, "wherever we decide to go. For now, though, until your baby is born it is best that we stay in Newport. All the nobs are closing up their cottages at this time, and when Aunt Letitia goes back to Boston I'll move in with you. Corinth is quite isolated, you know, hidden away from prying eyes, so we'll be safe."

I was delighted to leave everything to him, at least until after the birth, at which time I intended to have a voice in any plans. I was happy thinking about that, and happy in

Desmond's love, even though there was no possibility of our marrying. He was everything I had ever hoped for, handsome, charming, amusing, and crazy about me. Best of all, he was rich. What more could I ask? The only slight cloud on my horizon during those bright fall days was the fear that Leland would come and find me, that he'd appear in the night, that I'd wake up and find him standing next to my bed . . .

"Get one of the maids to sleep in the room next to you, darling," Desmond suggested, "at least until I move in with you. Tell her you need someone near you in case you feel ill during the night."

Jessie was only too happy to oblige, and my mind was somewhat more at ease. Things were far better, though, when Aunt Letitia finally went back to Boston and I could sleep in Desmond's warm, protective embrace.

I knew I ought to write to Caro and tell her where I was, but kept putting it off and putting it off until it was too late. The estate manager in Newport sent word that he had orders from Miss Prentice's lawyer (I guess Caro used the same one) to close up the house for the winter on the fifteenth of October, as usual, and the very day the notice arrived I lost Leland's baby. I'd gone out into the garden after lunch — it was a lovely day at the end of September — but when a mist began to blow in from the sea I started back to the house. I remember having a perfectly horrible pain, the worst I ever had, and suddenly feeling dizzy. After that it was all a blur, or nothing, until I woke up in my bed with a doctor, a nurse, and Desmond hovering over me.

I must say that I felt relieved. I had never wanted that child — or any child, for that matter — and I could tell that Desmond was glad to have the problem solved. As soon as I was well enough to be moved he took me over to his great-aunt's place, The Hide-a-way (what a ridiculous name for that huge shingled pile!) to finish recuperating.

"It's fine for a while," Desmond said one evening as we sat in front of the fire in the drawing room, "but even Aunt Letitia would think it peculiar if I were to spend the winter here. Where would you like to go, darling?"

"Someplace where Leland will never find me," I answered. "Far away from New York."

"We could travel," he said. "Spain, France, Italy, wherever you feel like going. Then when we find a place we like, we can settle down as man and wife. Who would ever know we weren't married?"

Despite my desire to put distance between Leland and me, I was nervous about leaving the world that was familiar to me. I even began to wish I were back with my parents and Caro and my brothers in the old house on Harrison Street. Everything had been so simple then; it had been such a comfortable, safe life, while now nothing and no place felt safe to me anymore.

Part VII

Caroline

Chapter 17

In spite of my concern for Laurel, not knowing where she was or whether she was even alive, the spring of 1895 was a happy time for me. I was finishing my course at the Normal College, I had the prospect of a teaching position at Miss Endicott's private school for young ladies, and best of all, John asked me to marry him. Brad's marriage to Elspeth would take place that summer, and after the honeymoon they planned to live in a larger apartment over on Park Avenue, which meant that John and I could have the brownstone flat until we could afford something better. All of these things combined to push worry about my sister to the back of my mind, where it stayed until her letter, a short note, really, came at the end of May.

She and Desmond were "deliriously happy," she wrote, in Neuilly, France, near Paris, and she had no idea when, if ever, they would return to America. There was no mention of the baby, which would have been born in February, so we assumed she had carried out her threat to leave the child on the doorstep of an orphanage, or else found someone to adopt it. As Brad had always insisted, Laurel was adept in getting what she wanted.

"Should we say anything about this note to Leland?" Brad asked when he finished reading Laurel's message. "He'll be dropping in one of these evenings, we can count on that."

Leland had become a fairly frequent visitor to the flat, never staying longer than a half hour, during which time he kept glancing expectantly at the door of the parlor as if he thought Laurel might appear there at any moment. He never mentioned her, nor did he ever refer to the night he forced me down into the cellar and chased me through the tunnel. He apparently had no memory of that dreadful experience, or else, as John and Brad suggested, he was doing a superb job of pretending he knew nothing about it.

"Oh, no," I said in answer to Brad's question. "I'd be afraid to tell him. You don't know what he might do if he ever went to France. I'm sure he would go, and he'd find them together. Remember what I told you about how he attacked Desmond in Newport?"

"I almost wish he would go to France," Brad grumbled. "It's so damn hard to put up with him. If we could have a decent conversation it would be different, but he just sits there. *Yes* or *no* seems to be the extent of his vocabulary. I don't see why you feel you have to be so kind to him, Caro, especially after what he did to you. He's not your problem."

Why, I wondered, was I unable to ignore Leland? Even though I dreaded his visits I simply could not let his ring at the door go unanswered any more than I could have turned away from a cry for help from Laurel. That's what it was: Leland was calling for someone, anyone, to help him, and who was there except me? Had his aunt, I wondered, had an ulterior motive in leaving Corinth to me? Did she hope that such a legacy would tie me forever to the Prentices, specifically to Leland? Or was it merely a generous gesture on her part, since she knew I liked the place and that Leland had never cared for it?

Whatever her motive, I knew I had to be kind to Leland even though I could never help him in his search for Laurel. The whole thing made me feel deceitful.

After a while Leland's visits became less frequent, and when they ceased altogether (a blessed relief, according to Brad) I phoned Gordon to see if he was ill.

"No, he's fine, Miss Caroline," the butler said. "In fact, he's working hard on his book. Drinking a bit, but not to excess; I can always tell. He seems better than he has been since Mrs. Prentice left, although I'm afraid he's becoming a regular hermit. He never goes out anymore."

"Well, at least he's safe in the house with you in case of an attack, Gordon," I said. "Has he had any lately?"

"Oh my, yes," he answered gloomily. "Several. I don't dare leave him. He's after me to take a night off, but I seldom do. I can't, you see. He's always on my mind."

"I don't understand it," Brad said that evening. "Gordon's devotion to Leland doesn't seem natural to me. What kind of man would choose to play nursemaid to an epileptic for years and years when there are so many other opportunities? He's not stupid; he surely has enough wits to find another position."

"Maybe not," John said thoughtfully. "He may be afraid to leave an easy berth, life in luxurious surroundings, afraid of ending up in a cheap room and working his fingers to the bone for a pittance. But I agree with you, Brad; there is something not quite normal about the relationship of those two. I wonder if we'll ever find out what it is."

We did eventually find out, but it wasn't until the fall of 1897, more than two years after Laurel had gone to Europe with Desmond. By that time Brad and I were both married and John was doing so well with his firm that he and I were looking for larger quarters than the flat provided.

I enjoyed teaching at Miss Endicott's establishment during the school year, and each summer I opened the Newport house. Under the terms of Miss Prentice's will any money from the trust she had set up could be used only in connection with Corinth, so the guests I chose to invite were enabled to enjoy completely free vacations. I generally spent July and August there, with John coming up for long weekends whenever he could get away from the office, and of course for his vacation in August.

Brad and Elspeth were frequent visitors,

so I was seldom there by myself, and when I was alone, rather than pining away for company I cherished the privacy. It gave me time to read, to walk, to garden, or simply to do nothing at all while enjoying Milton's "sweet retired solitude."

Aside from the telephone I'd had installed in the center hall, Corinth stayed pretty much as Miss Prentice had left it, at least in the interior. I did have the numerous shrubs and bushes that had darkened the rooms on the first floor drastically cut back or removed entirely, causing Anton to remark that now the house looked as if it could breathe. He tended the garden with the same slow care he'd given it under Miss Prentice's eye, rarely consulting me about which annuals went where or which perennials needed replacing. It was as if he knew what his former employer would have wanted, and that he intended to preserve her garden as a kind of monument to her.

I was not surprised, therefore, when this ordinarily soft-spoken, placid man turned almost angrily on Brad for suggesting that the broken column be either restored or removed.

"No, no, sir!" Anton all but shouted. "That must not be touched! Nor the plantings around it! This is how she wanted it to stay, and stay it will! The colors of the flowers change, but that is all."

"I guess I've been told off," Brad said ruefully as Anton turned his back on us and began to weed the colorful little bed of portulaca. "What about you, Caro? Do you like that marble thing as it is, lying in the middle of the garden?"

"Yes, I do," I answered, "in spite of the memory of Leland crashing down on it and hitting his head. For Miss Prentice it represented a link with the past, with her father, mainly. For me, well, I guess it gives me a feeling of continuity, which, for some reason I don't understand, is important to me."

I saw John smile when I said that, and knew what he was thinking: That morning, I had told him I thought I was pregnant — another version of continuity.

Our baby, John Samuel Rambush, was born in the spring of 1897, and that year, together with him, his nurse, and the old servants Miss Prentice had had for years, I spent the entire summer at Corinth. Before I left New York I phoned Leland. I had seen nothing of him over the winter, but had made a practice of calling the Prentice house at least once every few weeks. Most of my conversations were with Gordon, who always assured me that all was well there, but on occasion I was able to speak to Leland. He surprised me with what sounded like genuine enthusiasm over the news of Johnnie's birth.

"A boy!" he exclaimed. "That's wonderful, Caroline. I'm really happy for you and John. May I come over and see him some time?"

He came the next day, bringing a perfectly beautiful silver mug, which he said had been his.

"Aunt Henrietta told me my mother bought it before I was born, and I always hoped to pass it on to a child of mine, but of course that's out of the question. I'd like to think someone is using it, and you and little Johnnie are closer to me than anyone else, now that . . ."

His voice trailed off, and he stared silently down at the carpet, apparently studying its pattern. Suddenly he shook his head, as if to clear his mind of any unwelcome thoughts, and smiled down at the baby in my arms.

"Gordon tells me your book is nearly finished, Leland," I said when he looked up again, "and that your publisher is pleased with it."

"Yes," he said happily. "It's nearly done. You can't imagine how much reading was involved. Witchcraft has been around almost since time began, and so much has been written about it. Did you ever realize, Caroline, that in some cultures witches were — and still may be — held responsible for all the evils that befall man? Most witches are women, you know, and some of them go undetected for years. They don't wear pointed hats and ride around on broomsticks; they're far too subtle for that. I've found it all fascinating, especially the trials they were subjected to and the punishments meted out to them. A lot of it makes complete sense to me.

"Oh, don't look so shocked, Caroline," he said as he stood up. "My interest is not a morbid one. It's purely literary, the result of some pretty heavy research."

He turned for a final look at Johnnie and smiled again as he gently touched the tiny hand that was curled around one of my fingers.

"So you're taking him to Corinth for the summer? The sea air should be good for him, and for you, too, Caroline. You'll have a chance to rest up. I'll see you when you return."

I stood at the window watching him go

down the steps of the stoop, wondering if his life was as lonely as I imagined it to be. He almost tripped on the worn last step, making me think we really had to start looking for a larger, newer apartment. I hadn't felt like exerting myself over the winter, and John simply hadn't had the time. Maybe in the fall . . .

Leland looks quite handsome, I thought as I watched him walk toward the corner, and not for the first time I marveled at how little the horrible epileptic attacks had affected his appearance, which had changed hardly at all since I first saw him leaning over the wall to pet Caesar. Could that be some kind of compensation for the suffering he had endured over the years? I wondered.

I phoned the Prentice house as soon as we returned to the city in September, but Gordon said Leland was not to be disturbed; he was putting the finishing touches on his manuscript and was in a state of excitement.

"I'll tell him you called, Miss Caroline," the butler said, "but I don't know when he'll get around to phoning you."

He never did call, but on Monday of the following week Laurel did.

Chapter 18

With the exception of a few postcards from various resorts along the Mediterranean, we'd heard nothing from Laurel for more than two years, and I was therefore astonished when she announced that she and Desmond were in New York.

"I have to talk to you, Caro. You're still in the flat on Lexington Avenue, aren't you? I'll be there in an hour," she said, and hung up before I could ask any questions.

"Oh my dear," she exclaimed when I opened the door for her forty-five minutes later, "I know you'll help us — you will, won't you? Oh, where's Brad? Oh dear, where to begin . . ."

It took some time before she calmed down enough to tell me what it was she needed — or wanted — but after a cup of coffee and a plate of hot, buttered toast she was able to make a start.

"I'll come right to the point, Caro," she said, taking a deep breath. "Desmond and I

209

need a place to stay for a while, and I thought if the Newport house were just standing there empty . . ."

She paused and eyed me shrewdly over the rim of her cup, waiting for my reaction.

"I was about to have it closed up for the season, Laurel, but if —"

"Oh, that's all right then," she interrupted. "As long as the servants will be there we'll be fine. Is there more coffee?"

"Yes," I said as I refilled her cup. "I can have them stay on until the middle of October, as they often did when Miss Prentice was alive. But tell me, Laurel, what brought you home?"

"Oh, only until the middle of October? Well, maybe by then . . . well, I guess you'll have to know, although really it's my private affair. We had a wonderful time for a couple of years, first in the house near Paris, then down on the Riviera, where there were parties all the time, almost every night. A very sophisticated crowd, you see, with yachts and everything. They gambled a lot, and of course we had to appear at the gaming tables or we'd have been left out of things. It was all right at first, and then Desmond began to lose money. I always thought some of those men were too sharp. Anyway, he ended up practically penniless. I'm sure they cheated him. We had barely enough for the steamer; we couldn't even afford a first-class cabin. I'd already sold my diamond necklace to cover some of the debts and I even had to sell most of my clothes, lovely, gorgeous silks and satins, Caro. A woman at the pension told me where to go — a terrible, musty place, and the old harridan who ran it didn't give me half, not even a third, of what they were worth."

"I thought Desmond had a steady income from his grandparents' trust," I said when she paused to sip her coffee. "What about that?"

"Yes, he did," she said slowly. "Oh, I might as well tell you the worst. You see, he lost so much money at the tables, roulette mostly, and borrowed and borrowed thousands and thousands, and the men he owed money to became nasty. They weren't a bit nice; they threatened him with terrible things, and once they gave him a beating."

She shook her head as if she couldn't believe such a thing had really happened.

"Well, anyway, they forced him to authorize the trustees, some bank in Baltimore, to send the monthly payments — the money we lived on — to a numbered account in Zurich, where only *they* could draw on it."

"And Desmond did that?" I was shocked.

"He had to, Caro. They said they'd kill him *and* me if he didn't. He had no choice."

"You still have your hundred dollars a month, don't you, Laurel? Can you manage on that?"

"Oh, heavens no! We couldn't possibly. What we thought we'd do is to go to Corinth so that Desmond could feel out his great-aunt, maybe make a clean breast of things, throw ourselves on her mercy. He's her favorite, you know, and he says she reads nothing but love stories and that she's a romantic with a soft spot in her heart for lovers. It's worth a try, anyway. Maybe she'll advance what she was planning to leave him."

I didn't like her plan at all, not one bit, but I knew it would be useless to try to dissuade her. In the end I gave her what cash I had in the house and promised to notify the staff at Corinth of her arrival. When that was settled she went off happily, looking as if she hadn't a care in the world, and without inquiring about John or the baby. Nor had she told me what became of her own child.

"You had no choice, darling," John said after I had told him of Laurel's visit, "but I have my doubts about their future. You did tell me, though, that Desmond is quite a charmer, so maybe the great-aunt will be susceptible and hand over his inheritance. I certainly hope so."

Brad, when he and Elspeth came to dinner the next night, had a different reaction:

"What a mess Laurel has made of her life!" he exclaimed. "I'd wash my hands of her if I were you, Caro. I wouldn't trust her for a minute. She's not true to any one of us."

"But Brad," Elspeth said gently, "look how she's stuck by Desmond through all his troubles. She can't be all bad."

"More likely she's stuck with him," he answered. "If something better comes along she'll leave him in a flash."

"I doubt that, Brad," I said, putting down my napkin. "I think she loves him. Shall we carry our coffee over to the fireplace?"

Chapter 19

I had become accustomed to taking Johnnie out in his carriage on fine days in order to give Nurse Rogers a chance to take care of his laundry, and one lovely September morning when I found myself on Fifth Avenue and Sixty-seventh Street some impulse (or curiosity) made me go on up to the next corner for a look at the house we'd lived in for less than a year. Its recent sale had not, as Mr. Cadell warned us, produced any profits for my father's heirs; mortgage payments, fees, and debts had taken it all, but we had been prepared for that.

I stood for a few minutes on the opposite side of Sixty-eighth Street remembering the day we moved in, Papa's pride, Mamma's delight, my own despair, and thinking how little it mattered to that great pile of stone who lived there. Except for different plantings in the window boxes it looked exactly as it had when we arrived in the cab; even the lace curtains seemed to be duplicates of the ones Mamma had chosen, and I would have wagered that the furnishings were every bit as luxurious as hers had been.

Then I remembered the cellar. Did the new owners know about the tunnel, or the "connection," as Miss Prentice had called it? Were they in danger of a visit from Leland? Should I speak to Gordon? As far as I could tell he knew nothing about that awful night.

Suddenly I shivered in the bright morning sun, and after a moment or two I wheeled the carriage across town to Madison and Park Avenues and on to the safety of Lexington.

"Couldn't you come up here for a few days, Caro?" Laurel sounded upset when she phoned that same night. "Desmond had to go to Philadelphia, and it's awfully spooky here by myself."

"I thought his family had disowned him."

"Well, yes, they did. But when he finally screwed up enough courage to go see Great-aunt Letitia and ask her to help us out, he never got around to it because she told him that his mother is sick, at death's door, and keeps asking for him. So he had to go. Please come, Caro."

"Laurel, I just got back from there, not two weeks ago. Now, look, you're not alone in the house."

"The maids have left. They'd arranged for other jobs after you went, so only Cook is here and she's no help. She snores loud enough for the whole of Newport to hear all night long, and would never wake up if someone broke in."

"When is Desmond coming back?"

"He didn't know. Maybe in a few days, he said, or maybe longer. He'll probably have to wait until the funeral is over. The only good thing is that his mother may have regretted cutting him off, and will leave him something. In the meantime I am so alone! I sleep in the daytime when I know Cook is up and around, and then I'm awake all night. I hear such noises; this house is awful for noises. Can't you come? Or maybe I could come and stay with you? I could leave a note for Desmond telling him where I am."

"We haven't room enough, Laurel," I said quickly. "We're crowded as it is, what with the baby and his nurse."

"Oh, I forgot about the baby. Well, you could leave him with the nurse, couldn't you? Just for a short time?"

"No, Laurel, I couldn't. I suggest that you

stop sleeping in the daytime and get Cook to make you a hot drink before you go up at night. That should help you sleep, or maybe you should take a strong whiskey and soda upstairs with you and drink it after you get into bed. Try that, Laurel. I'm going to hang up now. I hear Johnnie crying, and it's Nurse Rogers's night off."

I didn't like refusing Laurel's request, but neither did I like the idea of being at her beck and call. She's not a child any-more, I said to myself, and even if she were she's not your child, Caroline.

She didn't phone again, but a few days later I received a postcard on which she had printed in bold letters:

I NEVER THOUGHT YOU COULD BE SO MEAN, CARO, AND IF I BECOME A DRUNKARD IT WILL BE ON YOUR HEAD. LAUREL.

At least she's able to sleep nights, I thought, propping up the card against the clock on the mantelpiece as a reminder to show it to John. The picture on the reverse side looked like a little painting; it could have been a view of the water from the veranda at Corinth, with a sailboat and a fishing smack in the distance — oh, how

217

often I'd seen that sight!

"Good for you, darling," John said, returning the card to the mantel after he'd read the message. "She's too clever to succumb to alcohol and sometimes a little helps. I remember my father having a nightcap regularly during his last years. 'It soothes the nerves,' he'd say, 'and sends me off into a kind oblivion.' Have you heard anything further from Leland?"

"Oh, yes, he dropped in for a short time this afternoon. The book is finished, and he seemed relieved, but at the same time rather restless, as if he were at a loss for something to do."

"That's not surprising, Caroline. He probably misses the writing. Perhaps he should start on another book."

"I suggested that, John. I even reminded him that once he'd thought of writing one about the way the Dutch lived in New York when it was still called New Amsterdam, but he said no, he had other things on his mind. I was about to ask him what they were when the telephone rang and I had to go answer it. I was afraid it might be Laurel again, but it was only Elspeth. She's pregnant, you know, and not feeling too well, so I had to talk to her for a while. When I came back in here Leland was standing at the window, rubbing his hands together. He left immediately, so I never did have a chance to ask him what he had on his mind. I doubt he would have told me, anyway."

No, I thought later, much later, he most certainly would not have said a word about what he was thinking of doing.

Part VIII

Laurel

Chapter 20

I honestly don't know how I got through all those days alone at Corinth. Of course once I realized that whiskey and soda insured a good night's sleep life became a little bit, but not much, more bearable. The trouble was that I seemed to need more and more Scotch (fortunately Miss Prentice had left a well-stocked cellar), and then the next day I wouldn't feel so good. I thought I'd better be careful, but after taking just one drink and spending a dreadful wide-awake night, I went back to the three or four I'd been having.

I wasn't really worried, though; I knew that when Desmond came back I'd sleep peacefully in his arms without the help of a single drop of liquor. It was all Caro's fault, anyway. She could easily have arranged to come and stay with me.

Then the weather changed; the house was always cool, even in summer, and by early October it was downright cold. Luckily there were fireplaces in most of the rooms, and when Anton came — he no longer came every day — he would see that the wood baskets were filled.

As time went on — and oh, what dreary days those were! — I began to worry even though Desmond wrote that he'd be back soon and that he had good news. I hoped that meant plenty of money. On sunny days, when Anton was there "putting the garden to bed for the winter," as he phrased it, I would sometimes find a sheltered spot among the flower beds and watch him as he wrapped the rosebushes in burlap or cut back the withered chrysanthemums. Then, when he left, I'd go indoors; no matter how benign the weather I was nervous at being out there alone. I simply could not help feeling that someone or something might be watching me. Ridiculous, I know, but one day I must have dozed off in the garden chair, and when I opened my eyes Anton had left. I panicked, convinced for a moment or two that someone (Leland?) was lurking behind the lilac bush in the corner of the garden near the wall. As I hurried into the house I remembered how when I was a little girl Mamma used to laugh at me, saying I had a knack for seeing "a bear in a bush." Perhaps I never lost that knack.

Cook didn't help matters at all when, later in the day, she asked me if I'd seen a man walking back and forth in front of the house. I hadn't, but her question was enough to ensure a sleepless night. I was afraid to drink more than a weak whiskey and soda when I went up to bed for fear of being murdered while in an alcoholic stupor. If I stayed sober I could at least try to protect myself.

So, instead of carrying a bottle upstairs with me I took a large carving knife from the kitchen, slipping in to get it after Cook had gone to bed. As soon as I had that wicked-looking weapon in my hand I felt immeasurably better. I don't want to kill anyone, I thought, or even disfigure him, I just want to frighten him and make him go away.

Even though I kept the knife on the outside of the blankets, within easy reach of my right hand, I lay awake, listening, straining my ears for the sound of footsteps until the sky outside my windows brightened. I fell asleep then, only to be awakened a few hours later by the loud patter of rain on the shingles.

It continued to rain all that long, long day. At times it beat so heavily against the windows that I thought they might break. They didn't, although some of them leaked a little. A sullen fire in the drawing room did little to dispel the gloom that settled down over the house like a heavy gray blanket flung carelessly over some unprotesting object. I thought I'd go mad.

Cook must have seen how miserable I was, for she did her best to cheer me up with her culinary efforts: For lunch she served a mushroom soufflé, so light and delectable that it could have appeared on the table in one of those elegant restaurants Desmond and I used to go to in Paris. Then for dinner she gave me chicken in a wine sauce, tiny parsleyed potatoes, and some kind of tasty squash dish, all followed by a creamy chocolate mousse. It was delicious, and it did cheer me up a bit.

It was almost dark when I finished my dinner and went into the small library across the hall from the drawing room to look for something to read. I'm not much of a reader, I never was, but I desperately needed something, anything, to help pass the time. I had just put my hand on a slim volume entitled *The Romance of a Lifetime*, which I thought might interest me, when a loud crack of thunder came so close that it made the old house tremble. I ran into the hall just as Cook dashed out of the kitchen, still holding the iron skillet she'd been cleaning.

"Oh, ma'am," she gasped, "under the bed — that's where we should go. 'Tis the only safe place — ow!"

A brilliant flash of lightning lit up the hall, followed by the loudest clap of thunder I ever heard, causing Cook to grab hold of the newel post at the foot of the stairs just as the door to the drawing room opened and the hunched, dripping wet figure of a man emerged. I screamed and started up the stairs, turning just in time to see Cook bring the heavy skillet down on his head with a resounding thwack.

We stood, speechless and terrified, unable to move, staring at the still figure lying face-down at our feet. Maybe we should push him out the door into the rain, I thought wildly. He might be dead, and if he is, then we can bury him in the garden tomorrow, and no one will ever know.

" 'Tis him, ma'am," Cook said in a hoarse voice, "him I saw walkin' up and down out in front. He's wearin' the same coat. Lookin' to break in, no doubt, and now he's done it."

At that point several things happened: The man groaned, Cook raised the skillet, ready to strike again, the thunder rumbled ominously, and then the man lifted his head. A moment later I was staring into the pale blue, shifty eyes of Roddy Cameron.

"Why did she have to conk me with that thing?" Roddy grumbled, touching his head gingerly. "I'll have a lump the size of a muskmelon for weeks."

"She thought you were a sneak thief," I said sharply. "And she was right, wasn't she?"

We were sitting close to the small fire in the drawing room, sipping the tea that Cook reluctantly had made before she went upstairs. I'd had a hard time convincing her that our intruder was someone I knew, that he was harmless, and only broke in through the French door in the drawing room by forcing the lock (he said it was unlocked) because he'd been caught in the violent storm. I don't think she believed me, but, muttering something under her breath about Miss Prentice turning over in her grave, she carried in the tea and left us.

"I am not a sneak thief," Roddy protested weakly. "But I am broke. I ran into Desmond in Philadelphia and he lent me some money, but not enough. From something he said — I forget just what — I thought you

might be here, I'm on my way to Boston —
I visit relatives there every so often. I don't
like 'em much, but any port in a storm. If
you can lend me a few dollars I'll get out of
here as soon as the rain stops."

"Will you take the little bronze horse with
you this time?" I asked nastily. "There it is,
right behind you on the piecrust table. We
thought it would be safer there than in the
hall."

"I don't know what you're talking about,
Laurel. What's a bronze horse got to do with
anything?"

"You took it, Roddy, when you came here
that summer. You know you did. And you
sold it to a shop in town, where we saw it in
the window. We bought it back, so you are
in our debt."

"Must have been someone else," he said,
wincing as he leaned forward in his chair.
"Oh, my back! I've sprained it somehow.
Probably when I slipped on those wet
leaves — look, can you let me have a fiver
or not?"

"No, I cannot. And I want you to go. At
once. See, the rain is over, the moon is out,
and you'll be able to see your way back to
wherever you came from."

"Of all the inhospitable — no, you can't
make me go."

"Oh yes I can," I interrupted, bringing out the kitchen knife (a small one, not the big carver) I'd put in my pocket while I was persuading Cook to make the tea. I held it within inches of his face and watched him turn pale, and as he struggled to his feet I had the satisfaction of seeing a look of sheer terror cross his face.

He's a coward as well as a thief, I thought when I'd slammed the front door behind him, and he won't dare come back here again. It wasn't until the next morning that I noticed the absence not of the bronze horse this time, but of the little silver owl that had stood at one end of the mantelpiece.

"Will you be stayin' here, ma'am?" Cook asked me after breakfast as we stood at the drawing room window watching the men Anton had brought prepare to remove a good-sized tree that had gone down in the storm. "I'll be leavin' day after tomorrer, the fifteenth, like always. Anton's supposed to close up the house then, but if you wanted to stay . . ."

"Oh, no, Cook," I said, trying to repress a shudder at the thought of being entirely alone among all the shadows and creaks of the old house. "I'll be going to New York, so Anton can close up as usual."

"Are you all right, ma'am?" she asked. "Yer lookin' a little pale like."

I was not surprised that I looked "pale like," for I was at my wits' end. I had no idea where I'd go — certainly not back to the Sixty-ninth Street house, and Caro had made it clear that I would not be welcome at her place — and I had no money. Dear Heaven, I thought, what am I going to do? Oh, Desmond, where are you? What is keeping you?

I moped around for the rest of the day; not even Cook's omelette aux fines herbes and crème caramel at lunch helped, and finally I went upstairs to lie down. I fell asleep almost at once, which wasn't surprising since I'd been up most of the night before.

I'd been dreaming about Desmond, that he'd come back to hold me in his arms while he stroked my hair, when I awoke with a start. A hand did rest on my head and then moved down to my upper arm, where it lay lightly at first but then tightened almost painfully as I struggled to sit up and push Leland Prentice away from me. He sat quite still on the side of the bed, smiling, not a nice smile at all. I don't know how to describe it except to say that it reminded me of the smile I'd seen on the face of the witch in our old book of fairy tales when she lured Hansel and Gretel into her gingerbread house.

"Don't scream, Laurel," he said, still smiling. "No one will hear you. I sent the cook off, told her she wasn't needed any longer, since I'd be taking you back home with me."

"How did you know —"

"Where to find you? Easy. You should not have sent that postcard to Caroline if you wanted to remain hidden away."

"I am not going with you, Leland."

"Oh, yes you are, my dear, and you are going to stay with me. But first, you are going to oblige me: You're my wife, Laurel, and I have every right —"

I screamed then, and tried to break away from the amazingly strong grip he had on me. With his free hand he yanked off the quilt that covered me and started to lie down on top of me. I screamed again, but he paid no attention, intent on trying to get my skirt up around my hips. I could hardly move, but I did manage to bring my right hand up. I thought I'd scratch his face, but he jerked his head to one side and my index finger poked him in the eye instead. He was too startled to say anything, and in the silence that followed I heard a door slam somewhere downstairs.

"Be quiet!" he hissed, clamping a hand over my mouth.

Almost immediately we both heard the sound of footsteps on the uncarpeted back stairs. In a flash Leland was out of the room, disappearing into the dimness of the upstairs hall. I slipped off the bed, pulled my skirt down, and was looking for a weapon to ward off the next intruder (I thought it might be Roddy Cameron again) when Cook appeared in my doorway.

"Are you all right, ma'am? I thought I heard you scream," she said breathlessly.

"Yes, you did, Cook," I answered. "A mouse ran across the rug — you know how I can't stand the creatures."

"Oh, is that all? Well, I come back fer some of my things. Mr. Leland sent me off so fast I forgot half of them. An' what about yer dinner? I'd started to make the pastry fer meat pies — there's plenty fer two, an' you have to eat. Where's Mr. Leland now?"

"I don't know, Cook," I said as calmly as I could, "but I do know that I don't want you to leave tonight no matter what he says. You're supposed to stay until the fifteenth, aren't you? And I'll go then, too."

She looked puzzled, but after a few moments she nodded and said she'd get on with the dinner. She didn't seem to think it strange, though, when I followed her down to the kitchen and sat in her rocking chair while she rattled pots and pans around, but she was astonished when I said I'd have my dinner on a tray next to the nice warm stove.

"An' what about Mr. Leland?" she asked.

"If he comes back in time he can have his dinner in here on a tray, too," I replied. "It's warmer than in that barn of a dining room."

Leland came in from wherever he'd been hiding just as Cook was removing the spicy-smelling meat pies from the oven. He said nothing about having sent Cook off — maybe he'd forgotten that he had.

"Oh, there you are, Laurel," he said quite calmly, as if he'd been looking for me (which, in a sense, he had). "Are we picnicking in here tonight?"

When I ignored him he drew a chair up to the old wooden table in the middle of the room and asked Cook to fetch a bottle of wine from the cellar. While she was gone he stared at me; I could feel his eyes on me even when I wasn't looking at him. After a few minutes he cleared his throat and began to talk about his book.

"You really must hear this, Laurel," he said. "Oh, wait a minute; come over here and sit at the table with me. I have so much to tell you."

I thought I'd better humor him, and as long as Cook was nearby I felt relatively safe, so I sat down opposite him and waited for him to begin.

"Now listen carefully, Laurel," he said slowly as he poured us each a glass of wine. "This is important — mm, that's a good wine. Now listen: There is a mistaken idea that the witchcraft in Salem was unique. It was not. Another mistaken idea is that there are no witches anymore. There are, Laurel, indeed there are. I know that for a fact. But Salem first: What happened there in 1692 was directly descended from what had been going on in England and on the Continent for centuries. Let me tell you . . ."

And tell me he did! As I ate the succulent pieces of beef and whatever else Cook had put into her pies, along with a dish of steamed vegetables, Leland talked and talked and talked, leaving his dinner untouched, and pausing only to refill his glass from the bottle at his elbow.

"You see, my dear Laurel," he was saying when I started on the apple dessert Cook put in front of me, "that entire witchcraft business in Salem started when two little girls named Elizabeth Parris and Abigail Williams began to act in a peculiar manner. They took to crawling around the house on their hands and knees, making all kinds of strange noises; they smashed precious crockery, trod on hymn books, and cried out that they were being pricked with pins.

"A doctor, called in by their frantic parents, questioned the girls at length and concluded that they were possessed, that evil spirits had cast a spell over them. After that not one, but four ministers were asked to examine the girls, and all four agreed with the doctor's conclusion.

"In the end the girls accused two women, Sarah Goode and Sarah Osborne, along with Tituba, a West Indian slave in the Parris household, of bewitching them. Interesting, isn't it, Laurel, that all three of these accused witches were women? Of course there were some men witches — wizards — but they're inconsequential. It is women, women, who are seduced by the evil one and persuaded to do his will."

At this point in his recital Leland became so excited that he knocked over his wineglass, spilling its contents across the table. He upended the bottle, and when he saw that it was empty he threw it on the floor and shouted for Cook to bring him another one. It occurred to me that if he drank all of that one as well he'd be too intoxicated to do anything but sleep all night. I fervently hoped so, but in any case I planned to take the carving knife upstairs with me when I could slip away.

"You see, Laurel," Leland droned on, "there have been male witches; you can see them in some of Goya's marvelous paintings, but his best ones are of women. Oh, when we get back home I must show you one he did in 1794 — I have a copy. These are all women, a group of witches with their familiars. They're sticking pins into images and holding a basket of dead babies to use in their orgies. No wonder they were burned when they were caught!"

Why is he telling me all this, I asked myself when Leland paused to drink more wine. Does he just want to keep me with him? Can he really think I'm interested? Why does he keep repeating that most witches were women? To frighten me, so that I'll cling to him? He's never told me anything about his book before — why now? There must be a reason; Leland always has a reason for what he does. . . .

"And that's not all Goya did," he continued. "He has another painting called the

Sabbat, or the *Witches' Sabbath*, in which the central figure is a goat — the Devil in the form of a goat — and a group of women are worshipping it. Did you know that a witch can change her shape? She can appear as a dog with horns, or a giant ape with wings — what's the matter, Laurel? Where are you going? Sit down. Sit down, I say."

He was becoming so flushed and excited that I was afraid one of his attacks was coming on. It must have been the wine, though, because when I sat down he simply went on with his lecture.

"Now, sit still, Laurel. Cook, another bottle! This one's nearly empty. Where was I? Oh, yes, changing shapes; this all happened, you know, and when witches were accused and tried they were invariably found guilty. Sometimes they were tortured until they confessed, horrible torture. I won't go into that. In some cases they were thrown into deep water as a test. If they floated they were judged guilty, and if they sank they were innocent. Most, though, were burned. Burning was best. Yes, yes, h-ah hanging an' b-b-burning. B-burn b-b-burn . . ."

Leland began to talk gibberish, which wasn't unexpected since by this time he'd drunk the better part of three bottles of wine. He shouted for still another, but Cook had long since gone upstairs. When no one answered him he picked up his plate of cold, uneaten food and hurled it at the stove. He stared at the mess for a moment or two, then gradually his chin sank down onto his chest, his eyes closed, and he slumped forward until his head rested where the dinner plate had been.

I slipped out of the kitchen with the carving knife hidden in the folds of my skirt.

Whether I had convinced myself that Leland was dead to the world for the night or whether I felt adequately protected with the big knife beside me I don't know, but I slept soundly behind my locked door until the raucous cries of the seagulls woke me at dawn.

Cook was up early, and when I went down to the kitchen she'd gotten rid of the mess Leland had made and was preparing breakfast. He was nowhere to be seen, but I was sure he'd show up, determined to drag me off to New York.

"Have you seen Mr. Leland, Cook?" I asked, watching her set out plates and cups on the table.

"He's in his old room, ma'am, the one

239

over the coach house. Used to like to sleep there when he was a boy. Miss Prentice didn't like it very much. He had a regular bedroom upstairs at the end of the hall, but she humored him, she did. Likely he had too much wine last night, and didn't know rightly where he was."

"How do you know he's there?" I asked.

"Thought he might be, ma'am, when I seen his door open upstairs an' the bed not slept in. So I went over an' looked, an' sure enough there he was, snoring' away, still in his clothes."

I can't stay here any longer, I thought. Caro is my only hope now. . . .

I decided to telephone her again, thinking she'd know some way of getting enough money to me so that I could leave here, but when I went out into the hall and picked up the receiver nothing happened. I jiggled the phone a few times before I saw loose wires dangling against the wall. They'd been cut with a sharp instrument.

Cook called me, saying breakfast was ready, but for once I had little appetite for her perfectly cooked French toast and shirred eggs. She didn't mention Leland's absence, nor did she say anything about his behavior the night before. I suppose that over the years she'd seen plenty of drunkenness;

I wouldn't be surprised if she'd come to expect it of men with plenty of money.

I toyed with the idea of asking her to hide me in her house or lodging, wherever that was, until Desmond came, but then how would he know where to look for me? Of course I could leave a note for him, but wouldn't Leland find it? I was about to tell Cook how terrified I was of Leland and ask for whatever help she could give me when the front doorbell rang. As she hurried to answer it I moved over, close to the back door, ready to run — I don't know where — if Leland came storming in.

"Yes, sir, she's in the kitchen, sir, havin' her breakfast," I heard Cook say, and a moment later I burst into tears as Desmond strode across the room and took me into his arms.

Horrified by my account of Leland's actions, Desmond moved quickly. He sent Cook off to order a carriage to come to Corinth as soon as possible, and while I packed my few belongings he stood guard downstairs, ready to deal with Leland if he appeared. It all worked out beautifully; I closed the door to my room and locked it from the outside, pocketing the key, so that when Leland returned he'd think I was still asleep and would sit down to wait until I woke up. That, I reasoned, would keep him from looking for me right away, and I hurried down the stairs. In less than an hour Desmond and I were driving over to his great-aunt's cottage, and I was telling him about Roddy Cameron's frightening appearance.

"Do you mean to say he broke into the house?" Desmond asked angrily as he tightened his arm around me. "And then asked you for money?"

"Yes, that's what he did. He said you'd given him some, but that it was not enough for him to get to Boston."

"I gave him fifty dollars, just to get rid of him, Laurel. That should have been enough for the fare to Boston, but Roddy's always been a spendthrift. God knows what he did with it — squandered it on high living, probably. Well, he'll never get another cent from me after treating you like that. I've a good mind to beat him up, and I will if he ever comes near us again.

"Now, let me tell you my news: I had a chance to talk to Aunt Letitia after Mother's funeral, darling," Desmond said as we rattled along, "and she was only too willing to have me use her cottage for as long as I wanted. She won't be there: She was planning to stay in Philadelphia for a few weeks and then head back to Boston. I thought we could live there for a little while, until we decide where to settle. Leland doesn't know anything about Aunt Letitia, does he?"

"I don't see how he could, Desmond. But tell me, do we have enough money to live on now?"

He smiled and said that under the terms of his mother's will he would never have to worry about finances again. "You see, Mother's father, old Mr. Grayson, made a fortune in railroads, and when he died Mother and her two brothers inherited it all. No, we won't have to worry about money, darling, and," he added, looking rueful, "I shall never go near another gaming table as long as I live."

"Where do you think we should go to live?" I asked after a moment or two. "We can't stay in the cottage forever."

"I was thinking of Boston, darling," he said slowly. "We could rent a house on Beacon Hill, and you could pass for my wife. Who would know otherwise? And Leland wouldn't be apt to find you there."

I nodded and said it sounded like a possible solution, but that night after we'd made

243

love and were lying in the huge four-poster in the guest room reserved for the high and mighty, I wondered if living in Boston would be like trading old Miss Prentice for Great-aunt Letitia.

Part IX

Caroline

Chapter 21

I remember how happy I was that bright October morning playing with Johnnie and watching his funny little toothless smile when I dangled a string of brightly colored wooden beads in front of him or made the stuffed dog John had bought for him squeak when I squeezed it.

All's right with the world today, I thought as I put him down for his nap, and then my eye fell on the silver mug standing on a table near his crib. I wanted to ask Leland if he would mind if I had it engraved with Johnnie's initials, and when the baby was comfortably settled I went into the hall and picked up the telephone.

"Oh, he's not here, Miss Caroline," Gordon said. "He left yesterday for Newport. Said he'd take the night boat and spend a few days there. I asked him if he had your permission to stay in the house."

"Newport!" I cried. "Oh, Gordon! Laurel's there, and maybe Desmond, and you know — oh, I'd better call her and warn her —"

"I tried to reach Corinth, Miss Caroline, but the telephone isn't working."

"Oh, Gordon, why didn't you go with him?"

"I wanted to, Miss Caroline, but he wouldn't have me. He got so angry I was afraid he'd have one of his spells, so I let him go."

"Today's the fourteenth; they'll be closing up the house tomorrow. Maybe Laurel has left — but maybe not, if Desmond isn't back. Let me think what to do. I'll ring you again when I've decided."

"The boat is too slow, darling," John said when I reached him at his office. "Let me see what connections I can make by train. I'll go with you, of course. Don't worry. We'll sort things out."

Although I knew Nurse Rogers would take good care of Johnnie, I didn't like the idea of leaving him alone with her. Suppose something — I don't know what — went wrong? Suppose a burglar broke in? There'd be no man in the house to protect them.

In desperation I called Elspeth, who said

she and Brad would be only too glad to come over and spend the night.

"Yes, of course we'll come, Caro. After all, aren't we Johnnie's godparents?"

John was unable to make any train connections that would help us, so in the end we had to take the Fall River Line boat and arrived in Newport early on the morning of the fifteenth of October. Long before the carriage carrying John, Gordon, and me drew up in front of Corinth I saw the smoke blowing inland and knew with a horrible certainty what had happened. A few minutes later I could see Corinth, or rather the remains of Corinth, the ruin of Corinth, and fear gripped my heart.

What must have been a tremendous blaze had died down somewhat, so that now only tongues of flame leaped erratically at the half-burned walls and rafters. Laurel was not in sight.

"It had too good a start for us to save it, sir," a fireman was saying to John when I caught up with him. "It's a total loss, I'm thinkin', an' only Mr. Leland Prentice is hurt, burned pretty bad."

"Where is he?" demanded Gordon.

"Where is Leland?"

"Out there in the garden, sir. Won't let anyone near him. Threatened me with some sort of club; doesn't seem to be in his right mind, if you'll excuse me sayin' it, sir."

But Gordon was off before the man finished speaking.

"My sister, was she in the house?"

"No one was, ma'am, 'cept Mr. Leland must've been. No, no one else."

"There, darling," John said, putting his arm around my shoulders. "Laurel is safe, she's bound to be. Come, let's see to Leland. He'll need a doctor."

I hardly recognized the man seated on the fallen column, rocking back and forth while tears streamed down his blotched, disfigured face. His hair and eyebrows were gone, his nose was bleeding, and his hands and what I could see of his forearms through the torn sleeves of his shirt were blackened. When Gordon bent over him, murmuring words of comfort, Leland paid no attention, but kept moaning, a dreadful, keening sound like a soul in agony, as he continued to rock.

"Leland, where is Laurel?" I asked so sharply that he jerked his head up and looked at me. "Answer me, Leland, where is Laurel?"

"Not here," he muttered. "Room locked.

Empty. She should have been there. Should have been burned — witches get burned."

"Did you set the fire?"

"Yes, to burn her. But I love her too much. Went in to rescue her, broke down the door — Laurel not there — the flames — I can't —"

He gasped for breath once or twice, and then, in spite of Gordon's supporting arm, toppled over sideways, so that his head came to rest on the never-changing acanthus leaves that had graced the top of the column on which he lay. At that point Gordon broke down completely, making no attempt to control great, heart-breaking sobs as he gently stroked Leland's ravaged face.

Chapter 22

It took me months to put the horror of what happened in Newport on the fifteenth of October out of my mind. I am not sure that I have succeeded in doing that yet, but at least I no longer feel panic rising in me every time a fire engine rumbles past us on Lexington Avenue. And I've stopped trying to get in touch with Gordon; I thought he might still be living in the Prentice house pending its sale, but since he didn't answer the telephone or respond to my notes I couldn't tell.

It wasn't until a cold, snowy February morning that we heard from him. He wrote to say he would like to pay a call on John and me the following Thursday evening.

I'll be leaving the city soon, Miss Caroline, and probably will not return in the near future. I do not want to go, though, without telling you "the truth of the matter," to use a favorite expression of Miss Prentice's.

If it is convenient for you I shall be along at eight o'clock on Thursday, February 23rd.

Sincerely yours,
Edward Gordon

He'd looked dreadful at Leland's funeral; I do not think I have ever seen a face as haggard, as grief-stricken, as Gordon's was that day. He was dry-eyed and in complete control of his speech and his movements, yet he gave the impression that he was holding onto life by a thread so fine, so tenuous, that even a whisper might cause it to snap. I could only hope that time would help him to come to grips with the reality of Leland's death.

When he arrived the following Thursday evening he seemed better, although he looked thin and his eyes had that tired look that comes from not sleeping properly. His voice was strong, though, and there was no sign of emotion held precariously in check.

"I was going to write all this down, Miss Caroline," he said when we were seated in front of the coal fire in the parlor and John had poured us each a glass of wine, "but when I tried to put it on paper I couldn't seem to get it right. I can say it better, and if I leave something out or if something isn't clear, you can tell me and I'll straighten it out."

"Yes, of course, Gordon," I said when he paused. "Is it something about Miss Prentice?"

"Oh, yes," he said quickly. "Without her, things would have been quite different, but others were involved. I'll have to go back a bit.

"Years and years ago Miss Prentice hired me as an assistant to her butler; Crocker was his name. He'd been with the Prentice family for a long time, and was getting on — rheumatics and that. I'd been a waiter in a men's club, but never worked in a private household. Crocker took me in hand and taught me how things were done, or how Miss Prentice liked them done, which was what she had in mind when she hired me.

"It wasn't long, maybe six months or so, before I knew everything about the house from the cellar to the attics, as well as all the duties of a full-fledged butler. When Crocker left — Miss Prentice pensioned him off so that he could live comfortably — I felt ready to take over. Oh, I was nervous at first, and I did make a few mistakes, but Miss Prentice was patient with me. She said that was only to be expected.

"The work wasn't hard. She seldom entertained, even when she was younger, and if she did, her dinner parties were small ones, never more than six or eight people. I did have to be ready to answer her bell at any time of day, but she was easy to work for, and always told me to take time off for myself while she was having her afternoon nap; generally that meant an hour and a half, sometimes two hours. The pay was good, I enjoyed living in such a first-rate house with all its expensive furnishings, and was, if I may say so, a contented man. How long things might have gone on like that if — well, it's no use speculating.

"Crocker had been determined to tell me everything he knew about the house, its inhabitants, and its furnishings, some of it entirely unimportant now. One piece of information, however, changed the entire course of my life. The poor fellow would whirl around in his grave if he knew what he'd done, quite accidentally."

Gordon paused and after taking a sip of wine, smiled as if lost for a moment in some pleasing recollection.

"You may think I'm a stodgy old man," he said, placing the wineglass carefully on the table next to his chair, "and it may surprise you to hear that romance, a splendid kind of romance, did come my way."

I was surprised, but dared not show it for fear of interrupting his train of thought.

"As I said earlier, my duties were not heavy, and I often had a chance to spend a half hour or even an hour in the garden behind the house. It wasn't much of a garden then, just shrubbery and stone benches, but it stayed that way until Mr. Leland took an interest in it later on.

"I was there one day, late April it was, enjoying the warm sun — we'd had a terrible winter that year — when I heard what sounded like someone crying. I looked over the wall, you know the one Caesar used to walk along, Miss Caroline, and saw a young woman sitting with a book in her lap. She wasn't reading, though; her head was bowed, and she held a handkerchief up to her eyes, obviously wiping tears away. When she lifted her head and saw me she gasped and, a moment later fled into the house, your house.

"I leaned over the wall and picked up the book, which had fallen to the ground when she rose so hurriedly from the bench. I took it inside with me, intending to walk around the block and return it at my first opportunity. I didn't sleep much that night; I kept seeing her face, her lovely tear-stained face, every time I closed my eyes. She was what the storytellers call a raven-haired beauty, with the deepest of blue eyes and a face — oh, I can't begin to describe it. I knew from what Miss Prentice had told me that she must be Miss Sybil, the daughter of Miss Prentice's sister, Lavinia, now long dead. She was, therefore, Miss Prentice's niece.

"I never did return the book. I couldn't bear to part with it, a slim volume of some of Lord Byron's poems. I read them all, even memorized a few, and took it to bed with me every night. I still have it, and I can still quote: 'She walks in beauty, like the night / Of cloudless climes and starry skies; / And all that's best of dark and bright / Meet in her aspect and her eyes.'

"I saw her again about a week later. This time she smiled at me across the wall and apologized for her abrupt departure the previous week, saying she'd been upset that day. While we chatted she told me that her name was Sybil Bigelow and that her husband was on the stock exchange. She said she'd grown up in that house and had explored every bit of it. She asked me if I knew about the tunnel, or the connection, as Miss Prentice preferred to call it. I told her I knew all about it, that Crocker had showed it to me and told me how it came to be there. Apparently many years earlier, long before anyone thought of living so far uptown, there was a plan, later abandoned, to bring water down to lower Manhattan by means of a series of tunnels, only a few of which had been completed. During the excavating for old Mr. Prentice's two houses this particular piece was discovered, and instead of having it filled in, he took great delight in having it finished off, chuckling at the idea of owning a mysterious passage.

"Sybil said she thought the old man must have been lots of fun, and that she wished she'd known him. Then she went on to say that no one in her house was fun to be with.

"She looked sad for a moment, but her eyes brightened up again when we spoke of other things. I shall never forget how young, how very young and lovely she looked that day as she played with the string of beads around her neck while we talked. I wanted the afternoon to go on forever.

"We met several times after that, on each occasion learning more and more about each other, and it wasn't long before she confided in me that her marriage was not a happy one. She'd been too young to understand why her father insisted that she marry Walter Bigelow, but she thought it had something to do with money. She was only seventeen at the time, and so accustomed to being the obedient child that she never thought of questioning her father. She said that Bigelow paid hardly any attention to her, and that she had begun to think that he saw other women when he went out at night. He wasn't rude to her, and did not hurt her in any way, but simply ignored her. Even on the rare occasions when he came to her bed she never felt that he really desired her.

"I was at a loss as to how to comfort her, and when I saw the tears in her blue, blue eyes I had difficulty in restraining myself from taking her in my arms. Of course that would have been awkward with the stone wall between us. I did lean over to pat her shoulder, though, and after letting her small white hand rest on mine for a moment she turned and went into the house.

"I think that was when I realized how deeply in love with her I was, and I also think she was attracted to me; I wasn't too bad looking in those days. Well, we went on meeting in the garden for maybe three or four weeks, until we had a spell of bad weather. She must have wanted to see me as much as I longed for her, because after it had rained for three days in a row a letter came from her suggesting that I go through the tunnel the next afternoon and meet her in the cellar of the Bigelow house. The door would be unlocked, she wrote.

"Of course I went, lighting my way with a candle, and when I opened the door at the far end of the dark passage Sybil was waiting. I took her in my arms at once; I couldn't help myself, and after a while she led me to an old sofa underneath a small barred window. She said it had once been in the library, and was much more comfortable than the leather one bought to replace it. It was comfortable, and the two of us sat there, arms around each other, until it was time for me to go back.

"We didn't make love, not then, but I'm almost sure we would have pretty soon if Miss Prentice hadn't decided to go to Newport early that year. Of course I had to accompany her; it wasn't until much later that I stayed in town with Mr. Leland. I usually enjoyed the summers at Corinth, but that year I couldn't wait to return to the city. It was the longest summer of my life, and when it finally ended I was terrified that Sybil might have forgotten all about me or that her husband had taken her away someplace. My worry and apprehension must have been apparent, because twice Miss Prentice asked me if I were feeling ill."

"Hadn't Sybil written to you during the summer, Gordon?" I asked when he paused to watch John refill his glass.

"No, and I didn't write to her. We had agreed that it might be unwise to do so, which is, I think, an indication of how we felt about each other.

"It was all right, though," he said with a slight smile. "I went out into the garden the first chance I had after we were back in the city, hoping Sybil would see me. I wandered aimlessly around for a while, and finally sat down on one of those uncomfortable stone benches, waiting impatiently for her to appear. I was about to give up, heartsick and despondent, when a window on the second floor of her house was flung open. She leaned out, smiling, and motioned to me to meet her in the cellar.

"I think I was there almost in less time than it would take to tell it and — well, I guess you can imagine what went on."

He sighed, and after leaning back in the chair with his eyes closed for a minute or two, began to speak again, softly and slowly.

"All that fall, and during the early part of the winter, we spent as much time as possible with each other, and then in February she told me she was pregnant. At first we thought we'd go away together, live in some other

261

city, but Sybil was feeling so miserable that we decided to stay where we were and let the world think Bigelow was the father. The world, or our world, believed Sybil, even Bigelow, since he'd visited her bedroom sometime before Christmas, on which occasion he was so drunk that he couldn't remember falling asleep as soon as he'd climbed into her bed. The question of who the father was never came up.

"The child was born the following November, and before Sybil died she named him Leland. You know the rest, I think, how Bigelow brought him over to his great-aunt, left him with her, and took himself off. Sybil's fortune, inherited from her mother, was left in trust for the child, and there was no way Bigelow could get at it. So he left."

"I was glad he did. My dear boy was far better off in our household, especially when the epilepsy showed up, than he would have been living with his father and grandfather. Miss Prentice was wonderful with him, and I am everlastingly grateful to her for making it possible for me to live with my son — all I had left of Sybil."

"Did Miss Prentice ever know the truth?" John asked.

"I have a feeling she did, or at least suspected it," Gordon replied, "but if so, she never said a word about it. Her manner toward me didn't change a bit, but that could have been part of an act she was putting on, you know, to save face, or the family pride. She was a very proper person, and it never would have done for her to admit that Leland was illegitimate. She must have been aware of the interest I took in him, but of course I never told her I was the father. I never told Leland, either; he died in my arms thinking I was only the butler."

His voice broke then, and no one said anything for a while.

"But he always knew how much you loved him, Gordon," I said when the silence threatened to become awkward. "And Sybil knew —"

"Yes, maybe," he said, "maybe they both did, but there's one thing I'm certain of: Leland did not know he had epilepsy, thank God. Miss Prentice thought it would be cruel to tell him. She was afraid he'd go looking it up in books, and that it would worry him. She knew that epilepsy was considered a disgraceful disease, like insanity, and persuaded Dr. Bellingham to say he just had 'spells' once in a while. I was glad she took that position. If it had ever come out that he had the disease, he could have ended up in an asylum, and you know what they're like.

"Well," he said, pushing himself up out of the armchair, "I must be on my way, but I have one question before I go: Whatever became of your sister, Miss Caroline? Did you know that except for my very handsome pension Leland left everything to her? He made the will right after they were married, and never changed it, not even when he thought she was a witch."

"That was certainly quite an evening for revelations," John said after seeing Gordon out. "Poor Gordon! A heart-breaking love affair and years of servitude and selfless devotion, leading to what? Nothing but a solitary old age. At least Leland remembered him in his will."

"He didn't seem at all resentful or surprised at Laurel's good fortune, did he, John?"

"Not at all," he answered. "Actually I'm not too surprised, either. Remember how Brad always insisted that Laurel would get what she wanted?"

Indeed, Laurel did seem to have everything she ever wanted: a handsome husband, substantial if not great wealth, and thanks to Desmond's stylish great-aunt, a secure place in Boston society. We traveled up to visit her in the spring (she says she'll never set foot in New York again) and on the way home in the train I told John that for the first time in ages she seemed like the gay, carefree Laurel I'd known before that fateful trip to Ford's Theater in 1893.

Laurel's place in Boston society, however comfortable and desirable it seemed at first, was not destined to last. Shortly before Christmas — I remember I was packing a present to send to her, wrapping a small silver reindeer in tissue paper — when Desmond's letter arrived. I put the package aside and sat down to read it at once:

Dear Caroline,

I am writing to you at Laurel's request. She is too upset to do so herself. There's no major tragedy, but what happened has not been pleasant, and has forced us to change our living arrangements.

In early October, the beginning of the

social season here, we were at a supper dance, a gala and extravagant affair. Halfway through the evening we both noticed that the other guests, while not exactly ignoring us, were treating us in a manner that was definitely cool. We were puzzled, but after talking it over later decided that their behavior stemmed from the fact that the party had been so very, very formal and put it out of our minds.

There was more to it than that, however: It wasn't long before there were no more invitations, and we even had to stop giving dinner parties ourselves. Too many regrets. I was puzzled, my great-aunt furious, and Laurel distraught. It wasn't until just the other day when I ran into an old school friend of mine that I found out what had happened. He told me that Roddy Cameron and his cousins (*very* proper Bostonians) had been spreading the story about how Laurel and I spent the night together in the lodge in the woods when we went on that horseback riding trip. Apparently that will never be forgotten.

The damage is done, Caroline, and I see nothing for it but to take Laurel away and settle elsewhere. Where? I don't know yet. I only hope we are not forced to pack up and move from place to place for the rest of our lives like the Flying Dutchman or one of those fellows without a country.

That's all for now. We'll let you know our new address as soon as we have one.

Sincerely,
Desmond

The following summer we went to Newport for the last time. Corinth, or what was left of it, had been sold to a builder, who wanted it only for its valuable waterfront property, and my signature was required on certain legal documents. The money realized on the sale as well as the trust fund Miss Prentice established for the upkeep of Corinth have been turned over to me to use as I see fit.

I'm glad now that I made that trip, although at first I couldn't bear the thought of seeing the place again. The house wreckers, if that is what they are called, had been at work, and what was left of the building was barely recognizable. In the garden, however, the neglected flowers struggled to survive, and for a moment their fragrance made me feel that Miss Prentice was standing beside me, telling Anton to transplant this and cut that back. The phlox that had always grown behind the broken column was just beginning to flower, and as my glance lingered on that memento of a long-ago trip to Greece a shaft of sunlight broke through a bank of clouds, spreading its warmth slowly on the ancient marble in a gentle caress.

The employees of Thorndike Press hope you have enjoyed this Large Print book. All our Large Print titles are designed for easy reading, and all our books are made to last. Other Thorndike Press Large Print books are available at your library, through selected bookstores, or directly from us.

For information about titles, please call:

(800) 257-5157

To share your comments, please write:

Publisher
Thorndike Press
P.O. Box 159
Thorndike, Maine 04986